MW00978787

WATER BORNE

By

John Little

A novel of a storm at sea, shipwreck and survival and discovery on the rugged west coast of British Columbia.

First published in 2013
By Lulu.com

ISBN978-1-300-05922-6

Other books by John Little

It's A Dog's Life
First We Survive
From Within
Embers

Books of short stories

LOOK BACK TO SEE THE WAY AHEAD
SUMMER SMOKE
RAMBLINGS, MUSINGS and OTHER
STUFF
STORIES AND POEMS FROM HERE TO
THERE
Or a continuation of "Ramblings, Musings
and Other Stuff"

WATER BORNE

A patrolling seagull turned from its search as it spotted something lying at the water's edge. It landed on a weed and barnacle encrusted rock. Was it food or just a bundle of rags? No definitely not just rags, it was human, a body but was it food?

The bird cocked its head and studied the form as it moved in a rocking motion with the tide and small waves breaking on the shore.

After a few moments, seeing no unnatural movements it hopped down off the rock and zigzagged in dainty steps through the rocks and sandy patches. It stopped frequently, studying the form. It stretched its wings and pointing it's head to the sky, it opened its yellow bill to call to others; then quickly stopped the call and keeping its wings slightly open it moved, closing the distance. Twice it jumped back then tentatively moved forward again. Instinctively it went to what it knew was the head; if there was a meal to be had the eyes would be the first target.

As it reached the body the bird cocked its head, a noise or was it just the grinding of beach gravel? It lowered its head and cautiously pecked at a finger that lay across part of the face

A groan emanated from the form and as the bird let out a squawk in return the man rolled away from the water and mumbled aloud.

The seagull squawked again and leapt into the air and on beating wings flew straight away along the beach then out over the water. It turned after a few seconds and once more calmly resumed its search for food.

PART I

Chapter 1.

The man remained in the spot where he had rolled to for several minutes, then lifted his head and slowly looked at the beach, the water in which one foot still lay then turned his head and stared without thought at the moss covered rocks protruding from a line of stunted trees and salal brush. His wet body started to shiver and as comprehension dawned he struggled to his knees, crawled to a log and forced his body to a standing position. The air was warm and the cold that was the cause of his shivering was a result of being in the water and the soaked clothes he was wearing. Either reason or instinct guided his hands and he started pulling off his sodden pants, his shirt and underwear. He had only socks on his feet and after a moments hesitation, sat and pulled those off as well. The morning sun dried his damp skin and feeling stronger he flailed his arms and stamped his feet on a patch of sand. Strangely the exercise fed strength into his body and his brain quickly started to function. He picked up his clothes and spread them out over the log, then naked as the day he was born he slowly started moving around the beach keeping to the sandy areas and when necessary onto pebbled patches.

As he moved about, searching for anything that he could use he started recalling the events of the last few days.

He remembered casting off from his own secluded dock after topping up his fuel tank and heading down the channel going south. He had gone for a half hour along the backside of a chain of islands then swung about and headed out into the open water. He had followed this route many times before on his way to the eighteen mile shelf; choosing a narrow pass between two islands he had swung and had run on a due west bearing for another hour then slowed and prepared, his tackle for trolling. The weather report the night before had called for intermittent southerly breezes and scattered cloud so he relaxed knowing that that in spite of the normal long ten foot swells he could concentrate on fishing.. He had fished for about an hour, for once with no luck so had decided to run northwesterly along the shelf to the far end where it rose from the deep water.

As he got underway he had noticed the black line on the horizon but as there was no significant cloud build up he mentally shrugged and concentrated on where he was going.

Just over a half hour later he slowed and once again put out his lines.

The scattered cloud that was there earlier had been replaced by a thickening overcast, he noticed that the black line was still off to the west and was noticeably closer.

Suddenly the rod on his deep fishing line dipped abruptly and the line was torn from the down-rigger clip. He grabbed the rod and started reeling until he had taken up the slack then carefully commenced the fight with what he knew was a big fish. He immediately knew it wasn't a salmon that he had hooked as instead of the frenzied jerking and line stripping of a spring or coho, the fish at the other end was quietly resisting by using its weight and occasional tiny tugs.

"A halibut, by God, Bob me boy." He muttered aloud. He backed to the boat's console and cut the motor then switched on the automatic cable retrievers on both down-riggers then bracing his knees against the gunwale he had set himself for what could be a long tug o war.

As he and the fish struggled he felt a breeze brush his cheek, he had glanced out to the west and saw that the leading edge of the black line was much closer but still ended on the horizon. Clouds were forming between it and the overcast which was now much lower.

"Might have to make a run for it when I get this sucker aboard." He had spoken aloud once more.

The struggle had gone on for a half hour, the fish had tired and the man, Bob, knew that he would prevail, another fifteen minutes had passed then as the fish finally started a desperate run the boat was pitched violently by a blast of wind.

Bob had stumbled and fallen against the engine cover, He had looked over his shoulder and had seen a line of cresting waves some half mile away. At the same time his line had gone slack as the fish took advantage of the moment and either threw the hook or broke the line.

Bob hadn't had time to worry about the loss of the fish, he rammed the rod into its travel holder and lunged for the console and the ignition switch.

As he had gotten underway the storm had hit, the rippled water had immediately turned into a frothing fury. The ever present rollers had grown in size and the distance between each crest had shortened by two thirds while seething wind waves whipped the oceans surface and heeled the turning boat!

Any thought of running straight for the distant islands had been quickly abandoned as a towering wave broke over the stern and flooded the cockpit with untold gallons of water.

The automatic bailer had switched on and a steady stream of water was swept away by the winds onslaught.

Bob had altered the boats direction so that the waves were hitting on the stern quarter, all too late he remembered that the twelve pound lead balls were still hanging on the ends of the down-rigger arms, but even remembering he had been helpless to do anything with them as he couldn't let loose of the boat's wheel.

At the moment he remembered, one ball snapped the steel line and instantly disappeared, the second continued to whip wildly until that line also broke and the ball hurtled into the boat and smashed against the hull next to Bob. He had grabbed it as it rolled and flung it over the side.

He had been unable to make any speed and had throttled back until he had just been making headway. The boat was still taking on water from the breaking waves and as the storm increased in intensity even more the bailer had failed to keep up and the water had crept over the floor boards.

The weight of the water had turned the boat sluggish and he had realized that it would eventually stall the motor. He had reached under his seat and struggled into a life vest, but couldn't tie it as he had to hold the wheel with at least one hand.

He had quickly lost track of time, he couldn't tell any longer if he was actually making headway as the boat had noticeably started to wallow. The engine spluttered then back fired, ran smoothly for a few moments then had suddenly quit. Without power he had been unable to steer and the boat turned in a passing wave and plunged straight down and into a trough. Water surged over the cabin and filled the cockpit and as the next wave hit the boat had turned sideways and then was rolled over as it tumbled down the face of the wave.

Bob had been flung from his seat and had suffered a hard blow to his head, he gasped and had sucked in a quantity of sea water then only half conscious he slid out of the cabin and across the side of the boat as the hull rolled to one side for a second then settled back upside down and started to sink stern first.

He had almost slipped out of the life vest but had remained aware enough to hook one arm and with the vest half on bobbed to the surface. Suddenly a few feet away the engine cover had suddenly popped to the surface, he had paddled to it and slid onto the top. The storm raged for several hours, as soon as he was able Bob had worked his other arm into the vest but his fingers were two numb to tie it properly. He no longer could remember much of what had gone on and realized that it didn't really matter he was here now.

As quickly as he shoved aside those first hours he wondered where is "here"? How long had he drifted and in what direction? He thought he had been at least two days on his tiny craft, he remembered that the wind had eventually ceased. But had he been caught in a current, had he gone northerly or southerly or had the wind and tide carried him towards the string of islands that stretched across his hidden cove?

It also dawned on him that it would be days or even weeks before anyone would miss him.

'But enough', he told himself; right now he had to find food and shelter, then perhaps later he could explore and see if he was on an island or somewhere that he might recognize.

Chapter 2

Having pushed the why's and where's into the back of his mind Bob continued his ginger footed search for anything he could use. What he desperately needed was something for his feet. He thought of putting his socks back on but dismissed the idea as quickly as it came. He looked up and down the small beach he was on then noticed at the one end that a short reef ran out into the water, 'with any luck there may be a better beach around there' he thought.

He made his way to and over the rock that stretched out and found a narrow gut that ran into the bush. He clambered along the water smoothed surface and in a moment found a slight bend in the channel; around the bend there was a huge pile of driftwood and other flotsam. "Bingo." He said aloud. "There must be something."

He picked his way over to where the debris started and immediately spotted several plastic bottles sticking out of logs and branches. He gathered them up and laid them together and continued searching. Soon he had accumulated a battered "jerry" can, several net floats, two boat bumpers – one of them rubber, a torn shirt and one leg from a pair of blue jeans, then searching where the brush drooped over the beach he spotted a red running shoe! It turned out to be two sizes too big, but no matter it would be invaluable.

Shortly after this find, he suddenly felt dizzy and he realized he had had no food or water all the while he was adrift. He donned the shoe and gathered his 'treasures' in his arms and slowly made his way back to his where his clothes were draped.

He staggered and plopped down on the log beside his clothes and rested while his head cleared once more. Then with an effort he started redressing in the still damp clothing.

He cinched the oversize running shoe tightly then folding the pant leg into a pad he tied this onto his other foot using strips he made from the shirt.

Then after another brief rest he walked to the waters edge and made his way over to one of the rocky outcrops. Almost immediately he was rewarded with the sight of a cluster of oysters jutting out from a corner of the rock.

He picked up a fist size boulder and smashed several of the oysters off their rocky bed then picking them up he laid them on top of the big rock and one by one smashed their shells. He picked away the broken shell bits and quickly stuffed the oyster meat into his mouth and swallowed without chewing. As soon as the last one was gone he continued his search and once more quickly found a second cluster. He realized as he finished the first few that in his haste he had lost much of the natural liquid, so this time he broke off the tip of the closed shell and slurped and sucked out as much liquid as he could before breaking his way into the meat.

He kept gathering oysters for a few more minutes but didn't eat anymore. He was still hungry but realized he could not afford to make himself sick and too much of the high salinity liquid along with too much food would likely cause just that.

He went back to the log and retightened his footwear then proceeded slowly along the beach in the opposite direction that he had gone before.

He not only searched along the last tide debris but also examined the high tide line just short of the bush and shrubs. For several minutes his only successes were more plastic bottles, a few sheets of old news paper and half a dozen plastic shopping bags. The most valuable find was a bundle of fish net. Everything he found, he carried along until he had an armful then deposited them at the bush line and marked the spot with a bag tied to a branch.

He didn't hurry and he slowly worked his way around a curve in the beach and out of sight of where he had come ashore. Finally he spied a glass wine jug lying on a bed of small water worn twigs. '*Glass!*' He could make a sharp tool and maybe improvise a better foot covering for his one foot. He laughed aloud!

As he stepped forward to retrieve the jug he noticed an opening in the bush and on closer examination he realized he had found a game trail. He followed it a few feet and then in a damp spot he saw a small hoof print. "Aha," he muttered. "Fresh meat if I can find some way to catch it."

Bob turned and went back to the beach and looking around he spotted a curved log that was in the full sun. He went and sat then leaned back into the curve. *"Gotta have a plan.'* He thought. *"I need shelter, food, a fire would be nice, I have to explore and see if this is a big or large island or an island at all.* For the first time he looked, really looked at the water out from 'his' beach. He saw that there were craggy rocks just breaking the surface and telltale signs of underwater rocks and then about a half mile away was another piece of land. *'How come I didn't see that before? Guess I never looked out at all, and I guess no boats will be coming through with all those rocks.'* As the sun warmed him he closed his eyes and gradually slipped into a light sleep.

Perhaps a half hour later he woke with a jerk. *'God, I'm thirsty.'* He thought. *'I should be doing things instead of sleeping.'* Nevertheless, in spite of his thirst he felt greatly refreshed. Wide awake and without further thought, he moved all his close finds to where he had dozed then made his way back down the beach and carried all those items back to the one spot. Finally he moved up the things he had left where he had washed ashore.

Once he had everything together he smashed the glass jug and using a shard he cut open the rubber boat bumper and fashioned a primitive moccasin-like shoe, he used it to replace the denim pad he had tied on.

He mentally flipped a coin to decide on building a shelter or looking for water. The latter easily won out. He made some more thin strips out of the old shirt and tied several of the plastic water bottles to his belt, then struck off on the game trail he had found earlier.

He made no attempt to be quiet; deer were not the issue right now, but their source of water was. In the

first few yards he found several salal bushes laden
with berries. He stopped and picked several handfuls
and crammed them into his mouth. They were not
overly juicy but there was enough liquid to give some
relief to his thirst and to ease his hunger that was re-
awaking.

Several times minor trails branched off but he stayed
with the most used trace, it soon became evident there
were more trails joining it going in his direction of
travel.

As he left the beach he noticed that rocky moss
covered humps started to become prevalent and on
several of these humps arbutus trees were growing.
"That's odd." He said aloud. "That means a
reasonably dry climate."

He knew that although slightly unusual it was still
consistent with occasional micro-climates on some of
the islands.

The rocky protrusions became more numerous and at
the same time the brush and timber growth changed.
Firs, some small and some quite large were growing
from crevasses and along the trail he was following.
As he rounded one outcrop he saw ahead several
hundred yards, one hump that was large enough that it
would have to be termed a hill.

The trail arrowed straight to the base of that hill.
When he got to within a few feet of where the hill
started to rise up, he found a clear pool of water!
There was no marshy ground, the pool was quite
circular and about three to four yards across. At the

edge he could easily discern a pebbly bottom but it appeared to deepen quickly.

He didn't hesitate, this was the watering hole for the deer, if they could drink it so could he. He dropped to his belly and lowered his lips to the surface. It was cold, very cold, it tasted fresh; his first tentative sip became a long gulping drink. He drank until he could drink no more, then rolled over on his back and stared up into the sky.

Chapter 3.

As Bob lay there, his mind carried him back to the how he had gotten into his present situation. He knew the storm was the recent instrument, but it was the accident of six months earlier that put him in a situation where he was alone and why a search for him was highly unlikely.

He remembered the night when a policeman had come to his door and quietly told him that his wife of two months had just been killed in a car accident coming home from work.

He remembered the funeral and the efforts of friends and family to provide comfort and understanding. He remembered his numbness and the zombie like days afterwards. When the idea came to him to quietly just leave everything and retreat to his cove he was thankful that because of his work as a consultant he could just up and go. And that was what he did, he sent brief notes to some of his closest friends and his brother that he was okay but would be going away for awhile, "I don't know how long." And that he would contact them when he got back.

As he lay there, tears started to form and for the first time; he cried. He called aloud, he called for his dead wife and he railed against the unfairness of her death. Then gradually the tears subsided and he slowly relaxed. He eventually got to his hands and knees, dipped his hands into the water and washed his face. He stood up and walked all the way around the pool. He had a brief thought of making some kind of a shelter nearby, but dismissed that with the realization that most of his food would be coming from the beach area and he did not want to force the deer and other animals to seek water elsewhere.

He washed out the plastic bottles then filled them with water and tied them again to his belt. As he retraced his steps he noticed that here and there were some patches of pine growing on some of the hillocks. He left the path and as he half expected found blueberry bushes growing amongst the pine. *'I need to do a berry bush inventory.'* He thought. As he approached where he had sampled the salal berries he noted that there were both high bush blue and red huckleberry bushes, close to the beach he noticed both salmon berry and thimble berry bushes were in a few patches but he had missed them earlier because they were a short distance off the trail.

He gathered some more oysters and piled them with his "booty" and deciding to beach-comb a bit more he continued down the beach.

Each time that he spotted a log that had obviously been cut by a saw he examined it closely, he had reasoned that one of them may have a piece of metal attached which was something he might be able to make into a knife.

He had only walked for a few minutes when he spotted something that looked familiar. Lying just beyond the water's edge was his boat's engine cover! He dragged it up to the edge of the bush, at that moment he had no idea what it could be used for but maybe some use could be found later.

Continuing with his search, Bob resumed his walk along the beach. He decided it must be in the mid afternoon so was not concerned about getting back to where his main stash was. Besides there were no comforts there and if he had to he could spend the night anywhere he stopped.

Within a hundred yards or so he spotted another familiar object, his life vest! Picking it up he slipped it on thinking that now he had something for a pillow or perhaps a small mattress for the night.

His search finally rewarded him with a broken two by twelve plank which when he rolled it over he discovered a piece of rusty steel about a foot long, two inches wide and a quarter inch in thickness. It was held onto the plank by two screws. He tried to smash it off the plank with a rock but to no avail. He sat back on his haunches and thought for a moment then stood and searched around until he finally found a thin flattish rock. He lay it between two more rocks and after several smashes with another rock he was successful in creating a narrow piece. He returned to the plank and using the rock sliver as a wedge he drove it under the chunk of steel and popped the screws from the wood.

"Now I got something," he muttered. "Wish I had a hammer and anvil."

Eager to get started on working the piece of steel he decided to turn back; when he reached the engine cover, he hesitated for a moment then picked it up. It was awkward to carry but he was now determined to get it back with everything else.

As he struggled along, he mulled over what he had found and what potential use each thing had. By the time he got back he had a few ideas and after a brief rest and a drink from one of his bottles, he cleared a spot against the bush line of wood chunks and large rocks then scraped up the driest sand he could find and using a couple of the plastic bags he carried the sand to the cleared spot and made a raised bed above the damper sand and pebbles. He went along the bush line breaking off branches from some of the small hemlock and spread them on the sand bed then he took the life vest and opened it up and spread it out at what would be the head of his bed. Lastly he placed the engine cover over the bed with the open end pointing out towards the water.

The day was almost over so starting to feel hunger pangs again, he struggled through the bush behind his new bed and after a few yards found the area to be more open than right at the shore line. He ate a few salal berries then picked more dropping them into one of the plastic bags. *'I didn't think these things would have any use,'* he thought. *'But you never know.'*

He spied some salmon berry bushes with a few late berries, these he ate as he knew that they were delicate and mostly a watery juice. After a short while he circled back and returned to the beach a short distance from his "camp". He dropped the berries beside the cover and walked down to the waters edge. During the early part of the day the water had receded with a minor tide then rose again to about where it had been when he regained consciousness. Now it had receded again exceeding the earlier low and an expanse of fine sand was exposed.

He walked on past several craggy rocks and out onto the tide exposed area, after a few feet he had been squirted twice from small holes in the sand. He went back, picked up the length of steel and returned to where he had been squirted and dropped to his knees. In a few minutes of furious digging he was in possession of four decent sized clams. He gathered them up and walked back to one of the rocks and knocked several oysters loose then went back to his bed.

He tried to open both the oysters and the clams with the piece of steel but immediately realized it was futile. He ended up smashing all of the bivalves as he had done before then settled back and enjoyed a meal of oysters, clams and berries. He washed it all down with water from the spring.

After eating, he pulled off his footwear and examined his feet, there were a couple of red spots on one heel and two of his toes but no blisters. *'I'll have to try and go barefoot and toughen them up,''* he thought. With nothing else to do and quite tired from the days efforts he crawled into his make shift shelter and was asleep in minutes.

A few hours later, as the colder night air settled in he awoke but having nothing to cover himself he could only curl up into a ball and wait for sleep to come once more.

Chapter 4.

Bob woke just at sun rise the next morning. He stiffly backed out from under the cover and finding a spot clear of rocks, he forced himself to do some vigorous exercises. Between the rising sun and his efforts he warmed up in a few minutes. He took a swallow of water, noting that he only had a half bottle left. He was already tired of raw oysters but having no choice he cracked open two that were left from the evening before and this time chewed them thoroughly before swallowing. As he sat and ate his breakfast he stared at the sun glinting off the rippled waters of the channel. Suddenly a thought struck him and he jumped to his feet, "Where did I leave it? It must be here." He cried aloud.

He went to his scrounge pile and quickly found the thick bottom of the broken glass jug. He laid it carefully on a log, pulled on his socks, his one shoe and the "moccasin" then picked up the newspaper pages and felt them. "They must be drier." He muttered.

He looked about and spotting a small branch projecting out from the bush, hurried to it and draped the paper over it.

"I need fines, maybe some pitch." He snatched up one of the multi-purpose plastic bags and headed to and along the deer trail. He hurried along until he was where the patch of pine were growing and leaving the trail he was soon shaking dead needles caught in the lower branches into the bag, When he felt he had enough he then moved over to one of the bigger trees and searched around the lower trunk. The first tree was all unbroken bark but a second one had several scars where limbs had broken off and he was able to scrape away almost two handfuls of dry pitch. One limb was still hanging by a sliver of wood, he broke it off and then broke it into several small pieces. Everything went into the bag and he returned to the beach.

He decided he should wait for a little while longer so walked to the narrow little bay where he had found the running shoe. He focused on one spot where because of a concentration of wood debris he had avoided the first time. Throwing the wood to one side he worked his way into mass of twigs, logs and water worn boards. His first find was a battered one gallon paint tin, the lid was still intact which explained its presence. Next came a piece of heavy plastic sheathing followed by a worn and tattered square of canvas. There were several more plastic bags and finally a tangled ball of nylon fishing line.

He spread out the canvas, threw everything onto it and after gathering the corners swung the bundle over his shoulder and made his way back to the camp.

He resisted taking a sip of the last of his water and set about making a rock lined pit. When it was completed he retrieved one piece of the hanging paper and crumpling it up he patiently arranged a small handful of the pine needles and sprinkled some of the more crystallized bits of pitch over the needles. Next he arranged some of the finest twigs from the pine branch in an open sided teepee shape. He fussed with everything a bit more then picked up the broken jug bottom. "God I hope this works. I know a magnifying glass will but is there enough in this?" He asked aloud.

He positioned himself to one side of the pit and leaned forward holding the piece of glass a short distance from the small pyramid. He angled it and twisted it, once as he moved his hands a bright spot the size of a finger nail appeared on the sand in front of the small pile.

Carefully if not patiently he twisted again and was successful in moving the spot onto the paper. *'Gotta get it smaller'.* Slowly he twisted the glass and gradually the spot reduced in diameter until it was no bigger than a thick pencil led. Almost immediately a brown spot appeared on the paper then blackened! He was afraid to move so he locked his arms and blew puffs of air at the expanding black area, a curl of smoke appeared then a tiny flame burst forth!

Bob put the glass to one side and carefully added a few more of the small twigs then gradually worked up to larger ones, within a few minutes he was adding some of the drift wood.

'Now for some steamed oysters." He thought.

He went down to one of the rocks and knocked off one large oyster, when he got back he placed it between the wall of the pit and the fire.

He turned the oyster several times, eventually steam started coming from between the two shells then they opened slightly. Bob quickly arranged a few embers so that the oyster was almost surrounded, waited a few minutes then wrapping one hand in a bit of remaining rag he pulled the oyster from the fire and set it aside to cool. In five minutes he sat back and relished the first hot food he had had in almost a week.

After sitting for a while, he stood gathered his water bottles and headed for the spring.

The trip was quicker this time, he didn't take any time to re – examine what he had seen before and he wanted to get on with more exploring and to see if he could find anything that would suggest where he was. He filled the bottles but left all but one beside the spring then picking up the trail again he struck off past the pool and followed a route that led around the bottom of the hill. Again other trails angled into the one he was following, a couple almost as well defined as the one he considered the main trail.

For the first quarter mile or so the scenery stayed much the same as what he had seen coming from the beach, then subtly at first a change in the tree species crept in, there was more fir, that gradually gave way to spruce and then suddenly was a mix of spruce, cedar and hemlock. Eventually the trail split and forked into two main trails. He hesitated for a second then struck off to his right and in a few minutes found that he was climbing a bit.

He contemplated turning and going back to take the other fork, but just as the thought occurred he spotted something that made him give a small gasp of surprise; there on a tree was the unmistakable mark of an axe! He looked ahead a few feet and yes, there was another and then another! He walked to the second one and looked at it closely; it wasn't fresh, but it had been there for awhile, perhaps ten to fifteen years he guessed.

All thought of turning back disappeared from his mind he picked up his pace and hurried forward, every few yards there was another blaze and then he noticed that brush and smaller trees had been cut and twice he found where an old windfall had been chopped out to provide for passage.

"No doubt about it," he said aloud. "Someone cleared this trail and I bet the animals have kept it open."

The incline was slight and he kept moving forward at a rapid pace.

Some fifteen minutes after noticing the first blaze he suddenly walked out into a small clearing; across the twenty feet of the brushed in opening was a roughly built log cabin!

Bob paused for a few seconds scanning the open space, he saw at once a small area that definitely looked like it had been cultivated at one time. There, just outside of the shack door a few feet was what had once been a fire pit.

Excited now by his find, Bob ran over to the half open door and pushed it wide open.

Inside was a mess; squirrels had obviously found it convenient as a storage area as there was a small pile of fir cones and discarded cone bracts and cores in one corner.

There was a rough bed made from small poles, several worn blankets were stretched across it; along one wall and centered in an end wall was a barrel balanced off the floor on rocks: from the top a stovepipe ran up to and out through the roof. A rough door with no hinges had been hacked in the front and the top had been beaten down so that there was a relatively flat area. A weathered square of ply wood was fastened to four poles, obviously a table as evidenced by a tin plate and a fork sitting on one corner, the one side was next to one end of the bed which must also have served as a chair.

Bob stepped on into the small room and started examining it and its contents in detail. In one corner he found a wooden box, it contained a varied assortment of things ranging from table utensils to a ball pein hammer to a mason jar full of nails and a few screws, there was more but he turned his attention to the rest of the room. Along the wall behind the barrel stove were clothes hanging on nails, a pair of rubber boots lying beneath them, there were two galvanized but rusty buckets on the floor next to the door. There were half a dozen pieces of what must have been fire wood stacked a couple of feet from the stove. He noted immediately that they had been sawn and not chopped.

There was a small four pane window set into an end wall on a slight angle.

'Better have a look around the outside' he thought, *'I can look at everything later.'*

Bob turned and went back out the door and went around to what he thought of as the back; there he found a lean-to built against the logs, with a quantity of sawn firewood neatly stacked. There was also a one man crosscut saw hanging by its handle from the wall and a shovel suspended between two large nails and a single bit axe set into a small chopping block. The handles of all three tools were somewhat chewed away. "Squirrels or mice", he said aloud.

Bob pulled the axe up and out of the chopping block, then after leaning it against the small woodpile, sat on the block.

His mind was in a turmoil; there was no doubt that the cabin was abandoned, he needed shelter but should he leave the beach? If he was to be rescued his chances were greater along the shore than back in the bush. While he sat mulling over his options he at first absently then alertly noted that there was a trail leading on into the bush from where he was, then he became aware of a noise. He couldn't put a source to the noise or even a probable cause. Shrugging it off he rose to his feet and sauntered over to where the trail entered the bush then on a whim he decided to follow it for a while.

Within minutes he arrived at another small clearing that had as its center piece a ten foot high pile of decaying branches and assorted sizes of chunks of wood, just beyond the pile there was another opening with nothing but sky forming the backdrop. He hurried past the pile and in a few feet found himself on a bank; somewhat less than two hundred feet below him was a rocky beach and beyond was nothing but empty sea and sky.

"Well that's open Pacific", he muttered. "More chance of spotting a boat out there than where I came ashore."

He stood gazing out for a few minutes, then speaking aloud again said, "Yep I'll move up, a coloumn of smoke is a coloumn of smoke no matter where and should be seen easier from here than on the on the other side."

He turned and retraced his steps. When he reached the cabin he hesitated then moved on back down the sloping trail.

When he reached the first junction he stopped then looked to where the sun was, it was still early in the day, he had a full bottle of water so swung onto the other fork. Fifteen or twenty minutes later he passed through the thicker brush that bordered the beach area and stepped out onto a log strewn rocky beach.

Picking out a convenient log, he sat and thought about what he should do next. He had a strong feeling that he was on an island and that whether he went left or right he would then have to arrive back at his campsite. There were salal berries all along the shore line so if he used up his water he would still have berries to suck juice from. *'Besides,* he thought, *'I'll just go for a couple hours and the if I haven't got there, I can come back and follow the trail back.'*

Bob jumped to his feet and headed off down the beach to his left.

Chapter 5

Once again Bob fell into the enjoyable role of a beach comber.

The rocky shoreline stretched out ahead in a gentle curve; hundreds perhaps thousands of logs, some in almost neat piles, others strewn about as though tossed like toothpicks by a giant hand covered most of the area adjacent to the bush line.

He quickly found that by walking on top of the logs he could make better time than clambering over the rocks even though, occasionally, he had to walk around those that were lying helter-skelter.

Also if he was to find anything of use to himself, it would be amongst the logs.

The first half hour passed with no significant finds, net floats were in abundance and he actually found two of the large glass balls popular with Japanese fishermen, these he moved back to the edge of the bush and once again used plastic bags as markers.

Finally he spotted a varnished spear of wood which turned out to be a wooden deck chair with one leg missing the last few inches. This he hung from a drooping alder branch then to make sure he also flagged it with another plastic bag.   *'My God,'* he thought, *'people and plastic bags are the worst pollution combination on earth.'*

A little further on he spotted the unmistakable stern of a small wooden boat sticking out from where it had been storm or tide driven into the alders and salal.

He jumped from log to log to the wreck but when he got close he could see that part of the bow was crushed in and the ribs had been caved in on one side. Never the less he stepped over the gunwale to examine the inside. It had probably been about sixteen or seventeen feet long. It had never had a cabin but the bow was enclosed by a small cuddy which was partly intact. Inside the cuddy he found a rusted tackle box and a rolled up rain slicker snagged on one of the broken boards.

He pulled both items out and quickly opened the catch on the tackle box. Inside was an assortment of lures, most of them rusted, but four of them in reasonable condition but most importantly in the bottom wrapped in an oily but fishy smelling rag was a filleting knife! Bob decided to keep all the contents of the box, there was nothing else in the boat, but fastened on the back was the remains of an outboard motor clamp.

He climbed back out of the boat and continued his trek down the beach.

The beach continued to curve back and in another hour he arrived at a point that had a reef running outwards into the water. Once around the point the beach changed direction and off in the distance he could see the island and the rocky passage he had found two days earlier. There were fewer logs and the shoreline was easier walking and in a short time he arrived at the spot where he had found his engine cover.

He figured it was mid to late afternoon, so he decided to follow as close to the bush line as possible and see what else the vagaries of the tides and waves had left behind.

When he arrived back at his camp he had a few more plastic bags, and his finds from the old boat. He had found a couple of short two by four boards and a four by four sheet of half inch plywood which he stored together above the high tide line.

The sun had set behind the trees but there were still a few embers in the fire pit which after adding some more fine twigs and pitch particles produced flames and he patiently added fuel until he had a satisfactory fire going.

His first inclination was to work on cleaning up the fishing lures but he knew that he had accumulated enough stuff that he had to devise a method of getting it all to the cabin. It would take too many trips if he carried it all by the armload.

He pondered the problem for a few minutes then jumped to his feet as an idea came to him.

He took the filleting knife from the tackle box then strode to and through the bushes, once through he looked about and in a few moments had spotted two small willowy trees that would serve the purpose. One was an alder the other a spindly cedar. He immediately set to work with the knife and in a short while had managed to cut both trees down. He started to drag them limbs and all when he shook his head, "no two to a side for strength", he searched about, found two more trees then headed back out to the beach and to his camp.

As he started to limb them he paused then shrugging slightly he traded the knife for his piece of steel and went down to the water. The tide was half way in so getting a few oysters was no problem but he could only find three smallish clams.

He took the clams and oysters back to the fire but as he set them down he noticed the paint can he had found the day before.

Bob pried the top off and considered himself lucky that only remnants of paint were still in the can and this was still in a liquid form. He turned the tin upside down into the fire and watched for a few seconds as the paint drained out and caught fire; the flames quickly engulfed the interior of the can. Satisfied he turned back to the chore of de-limbing the four saplings.

By the time he was finished the paint had been completely burned from the can, but not satisfied he scooped up some of the embers from the fire and kindled a small fire inside the tin.

While the fuel in the tin burned he arranged his poles on the sand in an elongated 'V' shape. He turned, found the pant leg he had found before and using the knife cut it into strips, these he used to tie the four trees together at the apex of the 'V'.

Dusk was deepening, so he decided to leave the rest until morning and get on with cooking his dinner. Picking up one of the branches from the cedar he slipped it through the handle of the paint tin then carried the tin down to the water, he waded out a few feet then dipped the tin and after a few moments gingerly felt it. The tin was cool enough to touch so he swished it thoroughly then moved little ways away and scooped up water so that the tin was half full. He carried the tin back to the fire and made a spot for it on one side of the flames and set it into the fire. Then remembering the lid, he picked it up and placed it on the fire at another spot.

A little later as the water started to steam he dropped in his three clams, hesitated then dropped in two of the oysters. "Never had boiled oysters before, but you never know", he muttered. He still had two more oysters and these he placed as he had the one the night before. He fished out the lid and dropped it onto the tin.

Just as full darkness enveloped the beach, Bob drained the water from what was now a tin pot and sat back to relish another hot meal.

He lay back afterwards and stared up into the sky. It was a clear night and the stars were shining in their myriads, the milky way was a white arch that stretched between his one horizon and the trees behind him. *'This isn't so bad, by this time tomorrow, I'll be under shelter, I got food and there's more to get, I got some tools, I bet there are people out there who would pay for an experience like this.'*

His eyes closed and as he felt himself starting to drop into sleep, he rolled over and crawled into his bed. The action did not stop sleep from coming immediately.

Chapter 6

Bob awoke early and went down to the water's edge, stripped his clothes off and waded out until the water reached his waist then ducked under the surface then stooped and picked up a handful of the muddy sand and scrubbed his upper body then rinsing his hands he did the same to his lower body.

The water was still cool from the night time coolness and as he finished his libations he shivered a bit. He then turned and launched himself into a shallow dive came to the surface and stroked vigorously for a hundred yards, turned and swam into shore until his hands touched bottom.

He rose and walked ashore then gathering his clothes he walked up the beach drying himself with his shirt as he went.

He decided to forego a breakfast, as another meal of shellfish didn't appeal to him. Instead, still naked, he pulled the tarp and plastic sheet off his bed and set to work constructing a travois with the four poles he had readied the night before.

He spread the plastic sheet across the poles first, then the tarp on top of the plastic. Next he wrapped the two around and under two of the poles. Then using the filleting knife he made half a dozen slits and using pieces of the balled fishing line from his finds of the first day as thread he bound the two materials to the poles, he continued along the one side until it was bound the full length, he then repeated the process on the second side. In about an hour he had his wheel-les barrow ready to go.

He didn't know if everything he had found would eventually be of any use but decided to take as much as he could. In the end the only things not piled on were the engine cover and a couple of boards.

He backed into the vee-d poles and taking one in each hand, headed for the cabin.

After a few hundred yards, he found that because of the weight of his load he was struggling to keep his two handles spread apart. He lowered the poles to the ground and after a brief search found two small trees with forked tops. He whittled them down and then tied them together so that he had a fork on either end about three feet apart. He wedged these between the poles a couple of feet behind his travois handles.

Before he started off he searched about and gathered salal berries and had his breakfast.

It took close to two hours to make it to the cabin.

Bob sat out in the small 'yard' and took a long rest during which time he thought about what his next chores should be.

Obviously he needed to clean the cabin as best he could then organize it in at least a temporary fashion so that it would be a functional home. It took him a moment then he realized he had just thought of this run-down cabin as a 'home'! He shook his head slightly then murmured aloud, "well maybe it is my home, I wonder for how long".

He decided everything that wasn't fastened down, he would haul outside and then after cleaning the place he would move back what he felt would be necessary. The few meager items only took a short time to move outside; no broom was found so he cut some willows that were growing in one corner of the clearing and made a make-shift broom from the leafy branches. It took well into the early afternoon before he decided that everything was clean and orderly enough, at least for the immediate future.

Although he had picked up the full water bottles as he dragged the travois past the spring, he picked up the two buckets that had been by the door and headed to the spring. The round trip took under an hour, but he had spilt almost half a bucket of water when he caught a foot on a root.

His breakfast of salal berries had long before worn off and although he had drank as much water as he could while at the spring, hunger pangs had taken over.

He remembered the spot that had appeared to have been cultivated and on investigation he found a half dozen scrawny potato plants and a row of carrot tops all overrun by grass and some salmonberry sprouts. When he scratched away the dirt from one of the potato plants he found a handful of small thumb sized potatoes. The carrot tops yielded large hair root covered carrots, most of them split along their length. He washed the potatoes and one of the carrots and wolfed them down. The potatoes were tasty but the carrot was strong and rather woody.

'The spuds must be volunteers from the original garden, the carrots have probably just been growing here since God knows when.' He thought.

The sun was still high in the sky but realizing that once it went down he would be unable to make a fire, Bob gathered some fine fuels together and utilizing the old fire pit he again make a small cone shaped pile with the twigs and using the broken jug bottom quickly had a small blaze going.

Once the fire was well established he added some of the piled wood from the lean-to and supplemented that with some semi rotten chunks he found on the edge of the clearing.

Although tired, he figured he could make it down to the beach and back before dark, he wanted to find some more oysters and envisioned an oyster stew for his dinner.

He found that oysters weren't quite as plentiful and most of the ones he found had grown flatter and tighter to the rocks, however he did find a half dozen that he was able to remove intact and then under a very large rock with an almost cave like hollow he found a large bed of mussels. He pulled about a dozen of these from where they were anchored and returned to the cabin.

When he arrived back there was still plenty of fire burning in the pit so he scraped a pile of embers onto the shovel he had found in with the wood and carried them carefully into the shack and deposited them inside the barrel stove, he added some slivers of wood and in a few moments had a fire going.

He went back outside and dug a couple more handfuls of the tiny potatoes, pulled two more hairy carrots then took them inside, washed them and cut the carrots into small pieces, next he half filled one of the pots the cabin had provided with water and added the vegetables, then placed the pot on the stove.

The box by the bed had amongst other things, yielded a screwdriver and with this he shucked the oysters and mussels and added them to the potatoes and carrots. While his stew was cooking, he went back outside and sat at the fire pit, the afternoon shadows from the setting sun had already given way to dusk and although the first stars of the evening were beginning to twinkle, Bob didn't see them. He stared into the fire that was now reduced to glowing embers. In his mind he relived the storm and his awakening on the beach, the events since then and as he did he felt a growing conviction that he should stay on this island (for he was sure that it was) and using what had been left and the ever continuing gifts of the ocean; survive, heal and perhaps live again.

He stirred finally as his nose relayed to him that the stew was cooking, he rose and went into the shack and closed the door.

PART II

Chapter 1

Bob trotted up the trail, a makeshift
packsack made from a piece of canvas and
strips of lawn chair webbing was slung over
his back. He stopped at the fork and picked
up the two full water pails he had left there
that morning. The light rain that was falling
felt good on his bare skin and although the
air was getting cool now that summer had
passed his body was warm from the rapid
pace he had set for himself.
Although trotting was out of the question
because of the water, he continued on up the
cabin trail at a fast walk
It was late afternoon, he had just finished
fishing from the reef after having
circumvented the island for the second time
that week.
Wearing nothing but a breechclout made
from the same piece of canvas that his
packsack came from and a mismatched pair
of thongs on his feet, his skin was tanned to
a dark bronze and with his a beard covering

his face and his hair starting to touch his shoulders; he had the appearance of a creature from some primal time.

When he arrived at the cabin he paused briefly to survey with satisfaction, the small garden, now cultivated and showing some signs of recovery. Along the sunniest side of the cabin he had constructed a cold frame and growing inside were half a dozen tomato plants that he had started from the seeds of a tomato that he had found on the beach. Likewise there was a small apple tree almost eighteen inches high that was the result of an apple also found on the shore. It was carefully staked and enclosed in a fence of sapling poles.

He set the pails beside the door then strode around to the back and taking off his pack he carefully dumped the contents out on the wood chips that littered the ground. Two nice rock fish tumbled out first followed by the cleaned carcass of a large dungeness crab, then the leaves and grass that they had been lying upon; moving to one side he shook the packsack, out tumbled four cork net floats, and a red canvas case with a white cross on the front. He hadn't taken the time other than to take a quick glimpse inside when he had found the case.

He was eager now to see what all would be in the case but he muttered aloud, "No first things first, lotsa time for that later."

He reached around to his hip where his filleting knife now encased in more of the canvas, it was hanging on a leather thong. He quickly filleted the two fish then after skinning the fillets carried the remains around to the front and dug them into the ground at one end of the garden.

Going back to the lean-to he tossed the cork floats on the wood pile then picking up the case he went back around and into the cabin. Bob opened the door of the barrel stove and nodded when he found that the ashes were still hot, he poked them with a stick and saw that there were still some glowing embers. He carefully built up the fire frowning as he did. "I can't keep wasting wood while I'm not here, and the sun is almost no help now, I need matches."

Once the fire was drawing well, he put on a pot of water and a frying pan, then turned picked up the case from where he had dropped it and carried it over to the table. From the color and the cross on the front he was sure his find was a first aid kit although the weight was rather more than he would have expected. However, band-aids and small bandages would be handy for the many cuts and scratches his body was constantly enduring.

The zipper across the top opened easily and he immediately saw that he had found something more than just a first-aid kit! Lying on top was a coil of eighth inch nylon rope, underneath was several tins which from their labels three of them contained canned stew, two more were salmon.

Feeling excited, Bob upended the kit, spilling the remaining contents on to the table top.

"Holy shit", he cried aloud as he reached for two plastic cigarette lighters. He flicked one of them and on the third try he had a flame, the other lit after four flicks.

He sat back in the deck chair he had found months earlier and stared at the scattered contents of the bag. Food wise, there was the stew and the fish as well as three packages of Kraft Dinner, four tins of sardines and three large chocolate bars; there was a small canvas first-aid-kit, a string rapped bundle of four inch nails and two six inch spikes, a folded sheet of plastic and most importantly next to the lighters was a sheathed leatherman knife tool. Lastly there were three paper back books.

He could hardly believe his luck. He needed matches, he now had two lighters, the tinned food would be a welcome break from the tedium of shell fish, crabs and fresh fish and the leatherman with its assorted blades and tools would be invaluable.

He opened the small first-aid kit to find it was a small rendition of what he thought the large case was going to be. There were a dozen band-aids, a roll of gauze, a roll of tape, a bottle of iodine, a packet of ASA tablets and a small pair of blunt nosed scissors.

He gloated over everything for a few minutes then pushed it all to one side and got up to cook his evening meal. He was tempted for a moment to not cook the fish and instead open a tin of stew but resisted the temptation, knowing that the fish needed to be eaten while it was still fresh. He did relent later and when the crab was cooked, he used the same water to cook a box of Kraft Dinner. The cardboard boxes had survived quite well so the case probably hadn't been in the water very long.

Later after his dinner, Bob lit a candle and tried to read one of the novels but the light was not adequate and after a few minutes he gave up and sitting back in his chair turned his thoughts to the coming winter. He was not concerned about the weather, he knew from experience that he would be seeing a lot of rain and there would be many days ahead when there would be a lot of wind.

The books and the food from what he now believed was a survival kit reminded him that the long evenings offered nothing in the way of entertainment and he wondered how long he could go on eating bounty from the ocean with nothing to supplement it.

There were at least four deer on the island but he was reluctant to try and trap or hunt them in any way. Over the course of the summer they had become used to him and often drank from the pond when he was present. *'I wonder if I should have lit that signal fire when I saw one of those boats or one of the airplanes.'*

It was so, he had seen boats passing by on a half dozen occasions and about once a week a small sea-plane passed by to the east of his location. At first he considered rushing to where the pyre of limbs and chunks were piled but always convinced himself that it would be too late by the time he got a fire going. After the first few times he quit making the excuse and ignored the idea of being rescued.

Once one small boat had come close into the beach below the clearing where the signal fire was prepared. He had spotted it just as he was stepping out onto the beach and had quickly crouched down then retreated deeper into the bush until the boat had gone.

As he contemplated his situation, a thought came to him; if there were deer on this island, there would be deer on others. If he could get to one of them and he had a weapon, he could have fresh meat and not feel any guilt about killing any animals he was beginning to regard as his friends.

"I can make a bow, I made them when I was a kid, arrows maybe a little difficult without proper tools, but I'll figure it out and I'll build a raft." He said staring at the stove.

Chapter 2

The next morning Bob awoke earlier than usual and after a sardine breakfast he headed out, swede saw in hand. The rain had stopped during the night but a blanket of somber clouds hovered a few hundred feet above him. Once again he was clad only in his breechclout and canvas moccasins, although the air was cool, he had no concern about staying warm enough. He set off at a slow trot.

His choices for wood for a bow were limited by the tree species that grew on the island, so he had decided he would find a small cedar and split out the heart wood.

It took only a few minutes to arrive at the area where the most cedar were growing but after an hour's search he hadn't found a suitable tree.

He reversed his direction and headed towards the spring, once there he, turned and headed in a direction that would take him through the middle of the island.

A short while later he spotted a smallish cedar growing in the shadow of several hemlocks and a large spruce. It was under a foot in diameter and had grown tall in its quest for more sunlight.

Unable to put in a proper undercut with his saw, he sawed three parallel cuts into the tree, then after breaking the middle chunk out with his knife he put in a slanted back cut and had the tree on the ground in a few minutes.

He only needed a piece about six feet long, he presumed that the best heart wood would be at the bottom, but carrying a six foot chunk with a diameter of about ten inches would be a heavy burden. So compromising he cut the tree in half then working from there he progressively worked his way towards the butt. When he was still some distance from the butt end the core started to show stronger definition, he moved down the trunk a couple more feet and sawed through once again. Now satisfied that he was in to the best area he paced off just over six feet and cut the tree again.

Bob sat down on the base piece of the tree and after a brief rest, stood the piece he wanted on end, squatted and tilted the short log onto one shoulder, picked up the saw and headed back.

After he got back to the cabin he spent the rest of the day carefully extracting the reddish core out of the white outer wood, then as evening came on he started shaping the core into a classic long bow shape.

The next morning, up early again, Bob went down the trail a few yards where there was a hemlock windfall just off the path. Using the saw he made partial cuts into the fallen tree and then with his axe, split and pried out several chunks. He repeated this several times, then stacked most of the chunks beside the trail and with the axe and saw took all he could carry and went back up the hill. By the time he stopped to have a late breakfast he had twenty to thirty roughly formed arrows slightly thicker than a pencil. Some of them he split along their length for about three inches. He took them all inside and placed them on the floor beside the stove and weighted them down with a piece of plywood and several pieces of fire wood. The rest of the day he spent finishing the shaping of the bow and preparing it for stringing.

Going to bed that night, Bob thought, *'Tomorrow I got to go fishing again and try and find that roll of steel line.'*

The next day he retrieved the spin casting rod from the beneath a tree near the reef; as he waded out on the reef he smiled as he recalled his excitement the morning he had spotted the rod and reel laying across the rafters near the door. Up till then he had fished with only a hand line with limited success. With the discovery came the

49

realization that there should be more lures than the single one that was attached to the line and he finally found several more wrapped in an oily rag and pushed into a knot hole in one of the building logs.

Within a few minutes he hooked an eighteen inch rockfish and carried it to shore. He hooked it on a branch where he left the fishing rod and started down the beach looking for the spot where he had tossed a small roll of steel down rigger line wrapped around a short chunk of two by four.

This was one of the few finds he had not flagged with a bag and as he had found it a couple of weeks earlier, its exact location was difficult to pinpoint.

A good hour later he found it but not until he had walked past it twice. "Another job," he mumbled. "Gotta establish marked caches."

On the way back, Bob searched for and found enough mushrooms to partially fill his knapsack, then picked a few red huckleberries as well.

After cleaning and filleting the fish he started a small fire in the rock pit and put the fillets on a wire rack he had made and left them to cure in the wood smoke.

For most of the rest of the day he worked on the bow and the arrows. He tested the flex of the bow several times as he finished the shaping, then using a piece of the steel wire,

he bent the bow leaving it in a partial curve.
He was afraid to bend it too much as it was
still uncured and he didn't want to over-do
the curve.
After a dinner of fish and mushrooms and a
couple of handfuls of berries he started to
work on the arrows.
While searching for the wire earlier he had
picked up several smallish rocks, all
relatively flat. He selected one that was
slightly rougher than the others and one by
one he smoothed each arrow turning them
constantly as he "sanded" them. By the time
he had done the last one it was dark, so he
put them again on the floor and replaced the
plywood and wood weight
The next day he continued the finishing of
the arrows, the final "sanding" was done
with a fairly smooth piece of shale like rock.
He spent an hour after a meager lunch
building a a pole platform over the rockpit
then carefully spread the arrows across
making sure they were well supported then
erected a long pole that leaned toward the
pit and terminated about a foot short. To this
he hung the bow by one end. After
surveying his handiwork and making a few
adjustments he started a small fire. He kept
it going through the balance of the day.
Having forgot about getting anything for
dinner, he decided to celebrate and opened a

tin of the stew and heated it in the fire
outside.
He stoked the pit fire with some green wood
and went to bed a little later than usual.
That night he slept restlessly. He dreamed
that the fire roared into life and consumed
his hard work and he dreamed that in the
morning the fire was out but the bow and
arrows had disappeared.
He stumbled outside the next morning to a
drizzling rain and to find that the fire had
died out. Three of the arrows had warped
but the rest and the bow other than being
wet were just fine. He brought them all
inside and placed them in a corner well
away from the stove and weighted
everything down with the plywood weight.
After an initial disappointment, he
rationalized that the "setback" may have
been providential as the curing process had
been slowed and he would now be forced to
wait a little longer. He still had no idea how
he was going to "tip" his arrows, so made up
his mind to work on the raft while he figured
out that problem.
He 'stewed' up the rest of the berries and
drank a cup of hot water for his breakfast
then gathered together, his axe, the hammer,
several coils of rope that he had beach-
combed and the spikes that he had found in
the box.

Although it was still drizzling the temperature was reasonably warm. He rationalized it would be better to go practically naked than be confined within wet clothes all day.

Bob crammed as much as he could in his knap sack then struck out down the trail, axe in one hand and two empty water pails in the other.

The pails he dropped at the pond as he passed by then encumbered only by the axe he broke into a trot.

He vaguely realized that due to his constant activity and diet that his physical condition had changed over the months and he was probably stronger and more fit than he had ever been before.

When he reached the other beach, he paused only long enough to slip off the knapsack then started selecting the logs that he wanted for the raft.

He looked for logs he wanted with fairly uniform diameters and not too large as they had to be rolled out and then positioned. Finding an adequate number didn't pose any problem as the tides were a generous supplier. The lengths were not critical, but anything over sixteen feet and under eight he rejected.

In the first hour or so he found six logs all ranging in diameter from about fourteen inches to eighteen inches, two of them were perched on other logs and were easy to roll out onto the sand and gravel. The other four he had to pry up and out of depressions they had settled into.

Once free and out on the slope of the beach they were all easy to roll further down, but then they had to be turned and rolled so that they all were close together, this proved to be more strenuous but by mid day he had them all positioned and lying tight together. The tides had for the last week been rather average so he decided to take a chance that they would remain so for a few more days and had positioned all of them just below where the tide had last retreated after coming in.

He took a brief rest while he opened and ate a couple of raw oysters washed them down with a bottle of water.

Back to work, he worked the rope he had brought in a weaving pattern of under and over each of the logs, he did this at both ends then angle spiked the two outside logs on either side, next using long sticks he windlassed the ropes as tight as he could twist and nailed the two sticks to what he was now proud to call a raft.

Realizing that intent on his work he hadn't noticed the passing of the afternoon, so he gathered up his tools, repacked the knap sack and headed for the trail. As he started to enter the beach he paused then turned and went back. Taking out his last coil of rope, Bob fastened it to one end of the raft and as there was no outcrop nearby he rolled a large boulder from the edge of the bush out onto the beach and fastened the other end of the rope to the boulder. Satisfied that his precaution would ensure that the raft wouldn't stray if he was wrong about the tide, he shouldered the knap sack again and headed down the trail.

Chapter 3

The next morning, Bob examined the arrows and the bow and felt satisfied that they were ready for a trial. He still hadn't figured how he would tip the arrows but was anxious to give them a try anyway.

In order to protect the arrows from shattering he fastened a pad made from a beach combed pillow and folded plastic onto a tree on the edge of the clearing.

He strung the bow with the steel wire and from a distance of about nine or ten yards he notched the arrow, took careful aim and let fly. The featherless arrow flew on almost level flight but missed the target by at least a yard and disappeared into the bush beyond.

"Shit!" Bob exclaimed aloud. He put down the bow and went to look for his wayward arrow. He searched in vain for a half hour then gave up.

"Back to the drawing board" he mumbled disgustedly. "Can't afford to lose them."

He put the bow and the arrows back in the cabin and the taking his axe, he went beyond the clearing and cut four poles about ten feet long. He dragged them back to the cabin and laid them on the ground in a rough square then tied the four corners.

Going back into the cabin he took down a pair of ragged coveralls from a nail on one wall as well as the pants he had discarded. He went back outside and into the shed where he had stored more plastic and a chunk of canvas. Using some of his supply of small nails he attached all the various materials to one of the poles and using more twine he suspended the pillow target roughly in the middle.

Finally he raised the frame into an erect position so that everything hung from the top pole. He leaned the frame between two trees.

As he started to prepare to launch a second arrow, he paused and then went back into the shed and dragged out several chunks and broken pieces of plywood, these he propped up on the bush-side of the frame but a few feet away.

His arrows were all blunt so he had no concern about damaging his clothes.

It wasn't until the fifth arrow that he finally hit the target. It hit with sufficient force that it made a deep impression and held its position for a couple of seconds before falling to the ground.

Encouraged, Bob launched a half dozen more, four of which struck his target.

He gathered up all the arrows that he had used, several of them had passed through the barrier and were lying at the base of the

second barrier, one he found had deflected
and was lying off to one side.

Bob moved to the far side of the clearing
yards from his target and backed into the
edge of the bush,, he was now close to
fifteen yards from the frame. The first
couple of shots he was low, the next one on
an over correction he shot over the frame
and then finally he put one arrow almost
dead center in the target. He gathered up the
arrows again and continued launching for a
good hour. By the time he was finished he
was hitting somewhere on his target four
times out of five.

"Good enough, Robin Hood me lad. We'll
do more later. Now I have to go catch a
couple of fish." He put his arsenal in the
shed.

Grabbing his knapsack from the cabin he
headed down the trail.

As Bob arrived at the beach, he heard the
sound of an out board motor. Instead of
stepping out of the bush, he crouched down
behind a moss covered log and peered out.
About a hundred yards off shore a small
aluminum boat was slowly cruising by, the
solitary figure in the boat appeared to be a
boy although a wide brimmed hat hid the
face.

The boy or at least the person was holding what appeared to be a piece of paper in one hand while the other hand steered the outboard.

Once the boat started to turn towards the beach then straightened out again and continued its course past the island. It was going away from Bob's fishing reef, so he held his position until he could no longer hear the motor.

Although at one point he had been briefly tempted to stand and step out onto the beach, he had resisted the idea and had remained motionless.

Going down the beach to where the fishing rod and old tackle box were stored, Bob kept a wary watch behind.

By the time he had reached his tackle cache he had relaxed, reasoning that it was just some wayward passer by and by the direction of travel would probably make for one of the inner islands or just continue on to where he had come from.

Normally Bob just used the same lure each time he fished but today he hesitated and opened the old box.

In the top drawer there was a tangle of old, rusty lures, *'should throw those away'* he thought, but as he took them out he paused, *'metal, they're metal, I can pound them and*

file 'em down.' "Yes!" he cried aloud,
"arrowheads!"

He left them in the box and changing his
mind about using another lure, he took the
rod and hurried across the beach to the reef
and waded out to his waist. After a half
dozen casts, he hooked the first cod and
after depositing it on the beach returned and
quickly caught another.

As soon as the rod and reel were in the
hiding spot, and the old lures were in the
knapsack Bob hurried back to the cabin.
He filleted the fish and buried the remains in
record time.

Then even though his stomach was
growling, Bob took one of the old spinning
lures out to the shed and using the hammer
and the head of the axe, he flattened it out
then with one of the axe files he started
shaping it into a triangle. At first it didn't go
well as to file and hold the flattened metal
was difficult. Finally with the axe, he made
a shallow cut in a block of wood and
inserted one edge of the metal into it then
continued with the filing, first one side then
the other. When he was satisfied with the
shape he filed for a few moments on each
side of the pointed end then using a stone he
finished the point. He was quite satisfied
that in the end it would be an adequate
arrow head.

Finally answering his stomach's rumblings he took a break and went inside to start the fire and cook up his fish.

After cooking and eating he hurried back to lean-to and made four more arrow heads. Anxious now to see how they would perform he took the heaviest one and after carefully splitting the head of one arrow he inserted the transformed lure and cautiously slid it into the split. Next, using some linen line that he had found hanging from a nail, he bound the arrow from just behind the metal head to over an inch down the shaft. Then using his knife he shaved and tapered the two split portions that encased the metal head. Standing up from the chopping block he admired his handiwork for a moment then shook his head and said, "No, not good enough. It might slip."

He thought for a moment then going to the woodpile he found a chunk of pine with dried pitch down one side. He scraped off the pitch and picking up the arrow he went around and into the cabin.

He rummaged around in a box in one corner and found a rusty tin can, he dumped the pitch particles into it then started a fire in the stove. Once warmth could be felt on the top of the stove he put the tin on to heat and waited impatiently for the pitch to melt.

Once the heat was sufficient the pitch quickly melted, he held the arrow over the wood box and using a pair of pliers he picked up the tin and as he slowly turned the arrow in his fingers he poured the melted pitch over the tipped portion and down onto the linen binding.

The pitch seeped between the split sides and the metal tip and as it rapidly cooled and set a reasonably strong bond was formed. The pitch that covered the linen provided a hard protective surface.

He took the arrow outside and after a few minutes tentatively tested the strength of the resin bond. Satisfied he said, "One more test." He fetched the bow from the shed and standing in the middle of the clearing he notched the arrow and let fly at his target. The arrow flew true, only a couple of inches off the center of the pillow, it pierced the pillow and continued onward.

"No!" Bob cried aloud. He ran over to the target and stepping around it he stared at his pants impaled on to a piece of plywood. He started to laugh, and yelled out, "She worked, by God she worked!"

The arrow had pierced his pants and buried half of the metal tip into the plywood, He had no doubt that the arrow could easily do serious damage to the game he was going after.

After carefully extracting the arrow Bob rushed back to the wood shed and one after the other tipped a dozen more arrows, he didn't quit until he ran out of daylight. Finally he gathered up enough pitch to do all that he had made.

Going inside he restarted the fire and while he waited for it to heat up he opened a tin of stew and put water on to boil. He smiled as he thought, '*going to celebrate tonight.*' He lit a candle, put the pitch on to melt and sat back. When the Kraft Dinner and the tin of stew were cooking he sat forward and under the flickering light of the candle he pitched the arrows then put them outside.

In spite of his earlier intentions, Bob was only able to eat half of the stew and a third of the Kraft Dinner. "Won't have to cook tomorrow night any way," he muttered.

He washed the few utensils he had used, then stripped right down and had a fast body sponge in cold water.

To continue the celebration he decided to go to bed and read a few chapters of one of the pocket books. Fifteen minutes after he was in bed, he roused himself enough to blow out the candle and immediately fell back to sleep.

Chapter 4

The next morning after a quick breakfast, salal berries once again being the main course, Bob went out side and standing in the same spot as the day before he shot all twelve arrows. His marksmanship stood up to the test with all the arrows hitting somewhere on the pillow but two of the arrows failed. One when the shaft shattered at the head and the other when the metal head slipped in its slot and fell out.

"No problem, that leaves ten and I probably will only get one shot anyway." He told himself.

He spent some time preparing a lunch to take with him, rolling up two blankets in a sheet of plastic and added a few items to his pack, he strapped on his knife and as an after thought picked up the axe. *'Oops, almost forgot.'* He thought, he went back to the wood shed and lifted down a single oar he had found on one of his beach combing expeditions. As he gathered up the bow and his arrow supply he snapped his fingers and muttered, "I should have made a quiver." He picked up the pack and after re-aligning everything he slipped the arrows into it along one side.

He struck out for the far beach stopping only to fill up several water bottles on the way.

When he stepped out of the bush a short while later, he felt a sickening lurch in his stomach when he saw the raft wasn't in sight!

"No, God no, don't tell me." He cried aloud. But as he uttered the last word he spotted it a couple of hundred yards down the beach. He hurried to the raft and immediately guessed what had happened. *'There must have been a higher tide and she drifted.'* He thought. *'And the rope dragged and got caught in those other rocks.'*

"Actually this is better, the one end is already floating and I'll be able to push her in." He laid his pack, the oar and the bow on the raft and sunk the axe into one log then left to go look for a pry pole.

By the time he had found a suitable pry and as an afterthought a long pole almost eighteen feet long the morning was well advanced.

The tide had risen another few inches making the launching quite easy. He waded out pushing the raft until the water was waist deep then he hoisted himself on board. Standing up he stooped and picked up the long pole and started poling the raft across the narrow expanse of water to the other island.

The bottom shelved downwards very gradually and he was able to use his pole for almost a half hour before the water was too deep to pole with any force. He shipped the pole and taking up the oar he put it into the water at the 'stern' of the raft and using the old fisherman's method of fanning and propelling without lifting the oar he continued to move the raft forward. After an hour on the oar he was well over half way across but the tide was now ebbing and he was being carried sideways by it as he moved ahead. Once he realized what was happening he altered his direction to angle across the tide flow and increased his speed quite dramatically. His biggest concern now was to make landfall before he crossed the end of the island.

The water stayed fairly deep until he was only a couple of hundred yards off shore and when he could use the pole once more he pushed straight into the beach.

The exertion and worry about getting to the island had drained his energy and once he had secured the raft he lay back and had a short rest. *'Okay, I'm here, now what? Maybe I should have just gone after one of my own deer. No this will be best. Gotta find a trail, find a hiding spot and wait.* His mind ran on, one thought after another.

Hunger suddenly hit him and he took out half of his meager lunch and ate it.

A little later, much refreshed, Bob secured the raft to a sand embedded log and taking his pack and bow headed along the beach in the direction of his original intended landing spot.

It didn't take long before he found a game trail coming out onto the beach. He turned and followed it for a short distance but when he realized it wasn't really well defined he retraced his steps to the beach.

He found three more similar trails in the next little while then he realized that they all appeared to enter the beach in a similar angle and then twice found tracks in sandy spots. The tracks for the most part were going in his direction of travel.

Eventually he came to a moss covered expanse of solid rock. The tracks had gouged a well worn trail in the mossy covering.

The rock itself extended from the bush and disappeared out into the water of the channel. The highest parts of the mounded surface was perhaps fifteen feet above the beach surface and appeared to extend a quarter of a mile or so ahead. Other trails in the moss joined the one that Bob was following and in a few moments he came upon a half dozen depressions and shallow crevasses. All of them held water! Bob knelt down beside one that appeared to be about a foot deep and scooping up a handful hesitantly took a taste.

Smacking his lips he said aloud, "A bit brackish; must collect here from the rain so maybe not any springs. Now where do I set up?"

He looked around, the closest small reservoir was perhaps fifty yards from the edge of the bush. *'Further than I've been practicing, makes it not for sure.'*

Bob walked over to the bush line, un-shouldered his pack and leaned it and the bow against a shrub then turned and headed back to the raft. This time he stayed away from the trails, keeping close to the waters edge.

After double checking the security of the raft he took the axe and headed back to where he had left the bow and pack.

As he approached the rock out crop he walked to the waters edge and in a few moments had found a half dozen oysters cling to the rocks. He knocked them off with the axe then continued on; the oysters clutched to his body with one hand and the axe in the other hand.

He continued on into the bush several feet; leaving the oysters and the axe he went back and retrieved the pack and bow then picking up the axe he proceeded several hundred feet further into the bush. He selected and cut down two small bushy balsam trees and then and armful of alder and willow branches. He dragged all these out to the edge of the bush then proceeded to wedge them into crevasses a few yards out in the open.

He went and found several short logs and chunks of wood and after packing them up to the cut bushes used them as support and props. Finally he went back into the bush and cut several armfuls of balsam and spruce branches which he arranged as a bed behind the wedged trees and brush.

He skirted around the water holes and examined his handiwork from several angles then went back re-adjusted a few branches. Shrugging mentally he said aloud. "It'll have to do, I hope the buggers are thirsty. At least I'm a bit closer than I would have been."

It was now fairly late in the day but still too early to go to bed and he reasoned that if the deer watered at night it was still a bit early. He had noticed a long stretch of pebbly beach on the other side of the rock out crop so decided to do some exploring.

He was back in an hour or so, happily clutching another oar with a ring oarlock attached.

He sat down behind the hunting blind, pried open a couple of the oysters and ate them with the leftovers from his lunch.

He laid out his arrows and made sure that he had a clear opening through the branches of the blind; as dusk came on Bob loosely notched an arrow and knelt to watch out through the opening. After a few minutes he started to stiffen up and realized that if he needed to do something different.

He arranged another hole at rock level on the corner that looked back in the direction of the raft then lying on his belly he started his vigil.

The first few minutes were easy but then he found he was fighting to stay awake. It had been a long tiring day and although he longed to give in to his body's demands he forced himself to stay awake by shifting and alternating between one peek hole and the other.

Finally full darkness descended and he unrolled his bedroll and sliding under the blankets, fell instantly asleep.

Bob awoke with a start, for a moment he didn't know where he was then remembering he rolled over. Something had awakened him. He started to rise then quickly moved so that he could look out through the lower hole. At first he could see nothing but the rippled waters of the inlet, some beach boulders and the rock stretching out before him. Then he heard a faint noise. A wheeze, a sigh? He didn't know but he did know that it wasn't part of the usual night sounds.

As he stared out he saw a motion, what he had thought was a rock was moving slowly up onto the rock outcrop. "A deer!" He breathed. As he watched there was movement from a second smaller shape behind the first.

He carefully rose to his knees and felt for the bow. The arrow had rolled to one side but he drew another from the pile and notched it into the steel wire.

Slowly he raised himself and as slowly poked the arrow tip through the upper peek hole and hardly breathing waited for the deer to arrive at the water.

Twice they stopped and looked around, the second time he thought the lead animal looked right at him and he quickly closed his eyes.

Finally with a low snorting noise the bigger one, the doe, moved right up to one of the small water holes and lowered her head to drink. The smaller deer moved to another and followed suit.

As Bob started to aim and pull the notched arrow back he caught more motion out of the corner of his eye. Another one. Another doe and she was alone. She raised her nose, sniffed the air then moved to a third hole and started to drink.

The last was the one Bob wanted, but she was angled away from him, the shot would be difficult. He refocused on the first doe but as he did the last one suddenly shook her head and twisted her neck as she reached with a hind foot and scratched at her head. She then shifted and stood broadside to the blind as she raised her head and stared down the beach.

Bob shifted his point of aim, pulled the arrow back, took a deep breath, held for a second then let fly!

The arrow flew across the expanse of rock and buried itself behind the shoulder of the deer. She jumped, her back arched she took a couple of steps then fell to her front knees and rolled over on one side.

The other doe lifted her head and stared at her prostrate companion, then lowered her head and took another sip. Then sensing something she made a small noise and with her fawn ahead of her, ran past Bob and straight into the bush.

Chapter 5

A couple of hours after Bob had gathered up his gear and started off, the same aluminum boat that he had watched two days earlier arrived back in the bay. This time it came straight into shore and the solitary figure steered the boat to one of the sandy spots on the beach.

This time there was no hat to hide the fact that the figure in the boat had long black hair and when she stood to step out onto the sand there was no doubt that the boat operator was a young woman and not a boy. She dragged the boat a foot or so up onto the sand then got back in and tilted the motor out of the water. Getting out again, she picked up a small anchor resting on a coil of rope and after walking up the beach, firmly planted the anchor behind a large boulder. She went back to the boat and picked up a worn pack sack she opened the top flap and pulled out a weathered looking piece of paper. When she unfolded it, there was a map on the folded-in areas. She twisted it about, lining the map up with the shoreline. She nodded slightly and whispered, "I knew I was right, this has to be the place." She slung her pack over her shoulder, checked the anchor again then walked up to the edge of the beach and turned and started following the bush line. It only took a few moments to find the trail that Bob had been using almost on a daily basis, she noted the fresh use and stopped for a moment then shrugged and moved on and along the trail. When she arrived at the fork a few minutes later, she looked again at the map and without hesitation took the path to the cabin. Up to this point she had walked along feeling only a touch of excitement but suddenly a wave of emotion checked her stride. Her excitement had increased but she suddenly fully comprehended that some one else had been here recently and in fact could be in the cabin at that moment. She looked around and spying a broken limb picked it up and hefted it.

'It'll have to do.' She thought.

She moved ahead but now cautiously, taking care to make as little noise as possible.

In moments more she arrived at the edge of the small clearing. She stopped and slowly looked around the clearing. She noted the resurrected garden, the staked tree and the general tidiness of the 'yard'. The cabin looked or perhaps felt empty.

Tentatively she called out, "Hello, hello the cabin." Then clearing her throat called louder, "Is anyone home? Hello, hello."

She waited and when there was no response she moved slowly across the clearing and cautiously tried the door.

It swung open easily and she peered inside. Standing in the doorway she examined the sparse furnishings, she saw that everything was neat and well kept.

"Well whoever he is, he is a neat squatter anyway" She murmured aloud.

The girl moved on inside and slowly examined everything in the room. She felt the barrel stove and nodded her head. "It's been out for awhile. I wonder where he is?" There was no doubt in her mind that a man was living in the cabin. She saw that the bed had no blankets and that there was no pack board or sack on the wall or on the floor.

He's gone somewhere, but for how long I wonder, hasn't cleared out; too much stuff is still here.

She sat down on the edge of the bed and pondered on what she should do next. The cabin had been built by her grandfather before she was born. She had only recently pieced together her grandfather's story from some recently found documents which had included the map she had found sketched onto a piece of brown paper.

She had planned for her search to last a few days, back in her boat she had provisions and a change of clothes, finding the cabin occupied was a surprise but as she considered it her property, she wanted to establish that right. She decided that she would wait for the interloper's return and have him vacate the property.

While she thought, making up her mind she absently stretched her arms and fluffed her hair in a typical female movement. She was obviously more than just a pretty young woman, she was perhaps in her twenties or early thirties. She had dark brown eyes and a chin that revealed determination. She was slim and her earlier movements had suggested an athletic body.

She sat for a few more minutes, then went outside and around to the back. She saw where Bob had been fashioning arrows and realized what he had been doing when she found a couple of broken shafts and a discarded lure conversion.

'Off hunting, I bet, probably staked out a watering hole somewhere' was her thought. She spun on her heel and went back around to the cabin door, she reached inside and grabbed her knapsack and slinging onto her back she set off at a trot back down the trail. She arrived back at the boat and quickly disconnected the outboard and packed it up the beach then going back to the boat she lifted the bow and dragged it above the recent high water mark, there she put the

motor back in the boat and carried the anchor and its rope to the bush line and tied the rope to a small tree. Still working with speed she gathered up a few pieces of driftwood and arranged them around the boat so that it wouldn't be easily spotted from the water.

Next she reached into the boat and took out a small canvas bag then grabbed the boats gaff hook from where it was fastened and lastly unfastened a fish knife and case and strapped it onto her belt. Re-shouldering her pack the gaff in one hand and the bag in the other she returned to the trail and once more broke into a trot.

When she arrived back at the clearing, she paused and looked about, then satisfied that nothing had changed she crossed to the cabin, went in and shut the door behind her.

Chapter 6

The girl, Alicia, dropped everything at the
foot of the bed, hesitated then dragged the
single chair over to the door. She opened the
door and pushed the chair into the open
doorway and sat down. Although it was
cloudy, there was no rain and she had made
up her mind that if it was at all possible she
wanted to confront the intruder while he was
out in the open.

After awhile she was reminded by her
stomach that she hadn't eaten anything since
early that morning. She got up, fished a
sandwich out of her pack and resumed her
vigil while she slowly ate.

As she chewed her thoughts slipped back to
the events of the past few months. She had
been working up the coast as a wildlife
technician, a job she had held in the ten
years since she graduated from college. She
had worked in many of the communities
along the British Columbia coast and for the
last year out of Bella Coola. She had
received a call about three months earlier
that her mother was seriously ill and she was
needed. She had immediately taken a leave
of absence and drove back into the interior
and then to the coast and made her way to
her home town of Ucluelet.

She found her mother at home dying of liver cancer. She had refused hospice, preferring to be at home rather than a hundred miles away. Alicia had immediately made arrangements for extended leave. Her father, a fisherman had been lost at sea the year she graduated from high school. Insurance money had paid off the mortgage on the family home and her two years of college. Her mother had worked as a bookkeeper for a local cannery up to two years ago when she retired.

The first few weeks after her return her mother had been fairly strong and they spent some time traveling about and beachcombing along the exposed westerly beaches. During these times her mother started to tell her things about their family past that had always been a non topic. She knew that her mother was part native but knew nothing about her grandparents. As a child she had been close to a great uncle and a great aunt who had both lived on the nearby reservation. It seemed that her grandmother had been the daughter of one of the hereditary chiefs, probably as a result of some privileges and an independent disposition she had been very willful. Late in her teens she had been given her own boat and spent days and occasionally weeks on her own out on the water and on the different islands up and down the coast. One day when she had been refueling at the dock she watched a young white man dock an old square sterned canvas canoe that was powered by a small out board. For some reason the man caught her interest and after he bought then loaded a few supplies into the canoe, she approached him and asked where he came from. The exact conversation wasn't known but apparently he had been less than polite and had let her know that it was none of her business. Used to having her own way, her grandmother had reacted angrily and words were exchanged. She terminated the "conversation" by grabbing a paddle from the canoe and throwing it out into the water. The man stared at her grandmother for a moment then moving in a blur he grabbed her and tossed her after the paddle.

He then turned, untied his canoe, stepped in and pushed away. After starting the outboard he angled to his paddle and scooped it up into the canoe. He headed down the channel without looking back. Several people had witnessed the whole thing and when her Grandmother pulled herself up onto the float she was greeted with laughter. This angered her even further but she controlled herself and without a word, jumped into her boat, castoff and started her motor. At first she just wanted to get away from the laughter but after a few minutes she swung the boat about and headed for the far shore. When she got close she looked down the channel and spotted the dot that was the canoe. She turned her boat, slowed the motor and followed the canoe. The small canoe made good time but it was still over an hour and many islands later when it turned into a short beach between two reefs. When her grandmother saw where the canoe was going she cut the power to her engine and let her boat drift about a half mile off shore. She watched as the man got out of the canoe, took off the motor and carried it up and into the bush. Next he dragged the canoe above high water and arranged some beach debris around it, in moments it looked just like a thousand other accumulations of drift wood. Next the man picked up his box of supplies and disappeared into the bush.

Her grandmother sat and let the boat drift for another ten minutes then she started the motor and headed towards the island but angled the boat so that when she reached the beach she was beyond the shorter reef and out of sight of the beach with the canoe. She beached her boat, raised the motor then secured the boat to a log, she headed to where the canoe was hidden and then located the trail that led away from the beach.

It was easy to follow and before long she arrived at a small opening that was almost fully filled by a rough cabin. She ducked behind a small tree and knelt down to study the cabin. A closed door was facing her as was a small window, she couldn't see any movement through the window but as she watched a curl of smoke rose out of the chimney sticking up from the peak of the building.

Alicia's mother's knowledge of the next events were very sketchy and she didn't know or at least recall how the man had become aware of her grandmother's presence but sometime later there had been another confrontation between the two. Her grandmother had evidently laid claim to the island, saying it was Indian land and that he was a squatter. He had apparently laughed at her and suggested she go get an eviction notice.

Her mother had said, "Your grandma said they had a big yelling fight, but somehow that passed and she had supper with him then went back to her boat and went home." She apparently stayed back at her home for a few days then went back to the island. Again her mother told her, "This time the white

man was glad to see her and they walked
about the island he told her he had come
from an island on the other side of the
country and had found this island a few
years before. He had built the cabin and for
money he sold fish to a fish buyer at
Ucluelet and sometimes sold huckleberries
when they were in season.

Alicia's mother again didn't know all the
details but eventually her grandmother and
Silas (that was his name) lived together in
the cabin and her mother was born after
awhile.

One day when her mother was still a baby,
they took the canoe and went for supplies.
They had bought extra gasoline as well and
on the way out of the harbor they stopped to
visit grandma's parents. While her
grandmother and mother went up to visit,
Silas stayed back to mix the fuel. Some how
an explosion and fire occurred and Silas (her
grandfather) was killed. Alicia's mother
always said that her grandmother blamed it
on some young men that were at the dock
that day.

Her grandmother and mother moved back to
the reserve but after a few months, left and
moved across the water to Ucluelet. There
her grandmother eked out a living doing
various jobs but often would take her

daughter and go back to the cabin for days
and weeks at a time.
Eventually Alicia's mother grew up,
finished high school then met and married a
young seine fisherman, Alicia's father.

Alicia and her mother talked about this story
many times as the weeks passed, but in spite
of Alicia's repeated questions her mother
could recall nothing more. One day after the
cancer had progressed, her mother said, "Go
up in the attic, I had forgotten but your
grandma one day gave me a wooden box
and told me to keep it safe. I just
remembered a few minutes ago."
Alicia had done as she was told and after
rummaging about found an old wooden box
pushed under the eaves. She brought it down
to her mother and they had opened it
together. Amongst the papers and notes
there was the brown paper map and a
witnessed document that stated that the
island known by the Indian name of
Go'nsay in the Sound known as Barkley was
given over to the exclusive use of Marcet
Aleuta the daughter of Chief Daniel Aleuta
and her heirs for all time. The document was
signed by the Governor General of Canada.
Marcet Aleuta was her grandmother's name.

The next day Alicia went to the local bank and deposited the document in a safety deposit box.

Chapter 7

Bob was elated. He went to his prize, pulled out the arrow then dragged her away from the watering holes. He took out his filleting knife and cut the doe's throat.

He went back and retrieved his pack and shouldered it then going back to the deer he took her two hind legs and dragged her across the out crop and down onto the beach.

At the waters edge he proceeded to open the carcass and pull out the innards.

He sliced off a piece of the liver and went higher up on the beach. He prepared and lit a small fire and roasted the several strips of liver over the open flame.

He went back to the deer, picked up the heart and the rest of the liver and headed along the beach towards his raft.

A half hour later he grounded the raft beside the deer and dragged it on board. He went back to his hunting blind and retrieved the oar he had found the day before.

Bob now had two oars, one longer than the other but decided that if he could fashion oarlocks he could use them and make better time. He thought about pounding the one oarlock in with a rock but as it was brass he figured it would break or at least bend.

He searched along the driftwood line and found a "round" of fir about eight inches thick.

He split it with the axe then proceeded to make four pegs. He sharpened one end of each then went back to the raft. One outside log had a crack running along the top for a couple of feet. He inserted and pounded in one peg then a second three or four inches away.

The other out side log didn't have any cracks and he broke one peg after a few hits with the head of the axe.

He thought for a few seconds then picked up a fist sized rock from the beach and setting the blade of the axe on the top of the log, he pounded the head with the rock, eventually getting the blade in a couple of inches. He then removed the axe and pounded the remaining peg into the log. He made another peg and pounded it in as well.

He looked about making sure he hadn't forgot anything then pushed the raft and jumped onboard. He set the oars between the pegs then knelt down and slowly started rowing the raft towards his island.

He didn't know how well the makeshift oarlocks would stand up to the rowing pressure so he rowed slowly and occasionally checked to see if they had loosened. They stood up to the task almost half way across when one peg popped out of the axe cut. He reset it and pounded it in again.

This time he made it to where the water was shallow enough so that he could use the long pole once more.

The tide had not been a hindrance and he beached the raft in front of the trail. He unloaded the deer, his oars the axe and his pack then poled the raft to the rocks the rope had tangled in the day before. He tied a new rock onto the end of his rope and lowered it down into the small cluster of rocks. As he was a few feet off shore he had to jump into the water and wade to the beach.

He then lifted the deer and put it across his shoulders but immediately decided it was too heavy. He lowered it again, cut off the head then after a moments hesitation, laid the carcass on its back and using the axe cut it length wise into two pieces by cutting the ribs along one side of the back bone. He completed the task with the filleting knife. Bob carried one half up onto the trail, returned for the axe and selecting a tree, cut off a limb just over head height, leaving a six inch stub. Next he cut along the back of the hind leg of the deer creating a slit just above the hoof. He raised the side and slid the slit over the branch stub. The side was now just clear of the ground.

He went back to the other half then unslung his pack and crammed the liver and heart into it. Then repositioned it on his back and stooping easily lifted the side and slung it up and around his neck, the center resting on his pack and shoulders. He picked up the bow and as he passed the hanging side stooped and picked up the axe and carried on along the trail.

Chapter 8

Alicia, totally lost in her reverie of her grandparents time and the last months with her mother hardly noticed the passing of the day.

Finally she returned to the present, "I must have been sitting here for a good hour." She said.

She stood up and stretched then jogged around the clearing to loosen and warm up. *'Maybe I'll light a fire.'* She thought. She had noticed a stack of kindling at the end of the stove so moving the chair back inside she went in and set about shaving some of the kindling then using a lighter that was lying on the table, she started a fire in the stove, slowly adding larger pieces of wood as it took hold. She had left the door open when she had come inside and as she closed the door to the stove and stood up she noticed a movement from the corner of her eye. She whirled in time to see Bob take his second step into the clearing, he was stooped under the load on his back and hadn't yet seen that the door was open.

Alicia whirled, grabbed her gaff hook and sprang to the doorway! At that moment Bob glanced up, he stopped dead in his tracks and stared for a moment then yelled out,

"What are you doing, what are you doing in my house?"

He let the deer slide to the ground and he strode across the opening.

Alicia took in his long hair, his beard and his bloody clothes and hands.

She raised the gaff and shouted back, "You stop, back off you jerk. Your house? You're a squatter and not only is this shack mine but so is this whole island!"

Bob stopped and then replied in an even tone, "You're nuts girl. I've been living here for months and you're trespassing."

"I don't care how long you've been living, er squatting here. This place is mine and you, bucko are the trespasser!"

They stared at each other for a few moments. Bob realized that she was older than he first thought and he couldn't help but think, *'she's damn pretty.'*

Bob was the first to speak again, "Look, I'm tired, I'm dirty and I'm covered in blood and I need to hang this side of deer. Can we put this aside for a little while so's I can get this thing hung and get cleaned up a bit?"

Alicia stared for a moment longer then nodded "Go ahead I just started a fire I'll put some water on to heat." She had no sooner said the words than she mentally kicked herself. *'Don't be stupid, girl. Don't go soft.'*

However she turned and as he picked up the side of deer once more she turned and poured some water from a bucket into the old enamel basin sitting on a wooden apple box. She put it on the stove and then put more wood on the fire.

She picked up her gaff again and leaned it against the foot of the bed, then sat next to it.

A moment later Bob stepped through the doorway. "I should skin that thing out first." He said half aloud.

Without thinking Alicia said, "You clean up I'll do that."

"You? You'll …" Bob stopped and shrugged. "Go ahead if you think you can." Alicia jumped to her feet and slipped past and out the door taking her knife from its case as she went.

She had hunted all her teenage years and the years she had spent as a wildlife technician had often required she dress out game.

She had the hide off and rolled into a bundle by the time the water had warmed and Bob had washed. When she went around to the door he was standing with his back to her, stripped to the waist. Looking at his body she realized that he was younger than what she had thought thanks to the abundance of whiskers and hair.

She stared for a second or two then stepped back from the door way. She waited a few seconds then shouted out, "Where do you want the hide?"

Bob slipped on a clean T shirt and came to the door, "When you get finished just leave it there."

"I am finished."

"How? You can't be."

He strode past her and around to the lean-to. Hanging from the rafter was the skinned deer, no superficial cuts and no hair on the meat.

He turned and glared at her then said, "Where'd you learn to do that."

"I learned when I was a kid," Then not to lose the moment she added with a straight look, "I'm good with a knife."

He grunted and moved past her. She followed him inside and taking the basin of bloody water, through the contents outside and poured more water to heat.

Bob mumbled, "Go easy with the water, I gotta pack it."

Alicia whirled from the stove, "You are a miserable bastard, aren't you? I just skinned your bloody deer for you and now you're suggesting I shouldn't wash?"

Bob glared at Alicia then angrily said, "Look girlie, I didn't ask you here, I didn't need your help why don't you just go back to where you came from and leave me alone!"

Alicia matched his angry stare and hissed, "I'll go for now, I had thought maybe we could work this out amicably but you are obviously too bushed to be reasonable so I will go, but I'll be back and when I do you'll be out of here."

"Better bring an army with you."

"It won't be an army, but I will bring the proof that this is all mine." She waved her arm in a circle. "And I'll bring an eviction notice that you'll recognize by its long barrel." Alicia snatched up her knapsack and walked out and over to the trail head. Once she was out of sight she broke into a run. Bob stared after her then said aloud, "Stupid bitch. She's probably ticked 'cause I caught her snooping."

He paced around for a few moments then aloud again, "Ah to hell with it, I may as well get the rest of the thing before it gets dark."

He headed down the trail and when he reached the fork broke into a trot.

Chapter 9

When Alicia got back to the beach she pushed her boat out into the water lowered the motor, started it and making a quick turn set off for Ucluelet almost two hours away. As she planed along, she started to shake and a let out a few sobs. Tears ran down her cheeks until she angrily wiped them away, she shouted out "Stupid, stupid; I'll show him. It is mine, it is mine."

She hunched over the tiller arm and stared into the deepening shadows.

When Alicia awoke the next morning her first thought was to go back that day but after thinking over a couple of cups of coffee she decided to get well prepared and wait a few days. *'Besides let him think that I'm not coming back, then he will have let down his guard.'*

That morning she went to the bank and after taking out the old document she went to the town's only Notary Public. She explained that she wanted a photocopy and that the copy would be notarized as a true copy of the original, she also had the same thing done with the old map. Later she went to a marine supply store and purchased a chart of the Barkley Sound area and encircled the small island that the chart identified as Captains (Go'nsay) Island.

She made photocopies of her birth certificate and that of her mother's. Her mother's certificate identified that she was the daughter of Silas Ferguson and Marcet Aleuta.

Later she went to the RCMP office and asked if there had been reports about any white men living out on the islands, the answer was in the negative but as she was leaving a Missing Person poster caught her eye.

The poster was requesting information on "Robert (Bob) Anson age thirty seven. Last seen in March and was believed to have been living on Hubbard Island in the waters north of Tofino.

It described him as being five foot eleven, weight a hundred and ninety pounds. The photo was of a clean shaven good looking man. A separate paragraph said that his boat an eighteen foot Double Eagle, white hull was also missing.

It gave a phone number of a Jim Anson. She couldn't match the face in the picture to the hairy headed man of yesterday's encounter and she knew from seeing him shirtless that there must be thirty pounds different in weight, but still there was a nagging feeling that it just could be…..

She went back to the counter and asked if they could photocopy the poster. When the

clerk had a questioning look she said, "I'll
be traveling around the islands quite a bit
and you never know."

The clerk nodded and made her a copy.

All the paper work had been a slow process
and late afternoon was on her when she
returned to her home.

Later she made herself a meager meal then
on a whim poured herself a glass of wine
and a little later a second.

That night she dreamed of her grandmother
and men with hairy faces. She dreamed of a
violent storm then awoke in the early hours
of the morning to the sound of wind howling
past the corners of the eaves and the sound
of rain beating on the roof and windows.

The storm lasted for two days and even
though Alicia had decided not to hurry back,
by the third day she was pacing her floors
and made several trips down to the float
where her boat was tied.

That day she spent in selecting supplies and
packing them in two plastic wrapped boxes.
She dug out her old pup tent and sleeping
bag, then selected two changes of clothes.
She rolled all her papers and put them into a
around aluminum fishing rod holder with a
screw top. Lastly she went into the bedroom
that her mother had used and going to the
closet she reached into a corner and pulled
out a sheathed 30-30 Winchester carbine.

From the shelf she brought down a full box of cartridges.

The gun had originally been her father's but it had been hers since she was sixteen years of age.

Alicia laid everything out on the floor, double checked it all then prepared her dinner. That night she went to bed at nine o'clock after setting her alarm for four a.m.

By five the next morning Alicia was stripping off her boat cover. She unloaded her car, placed everything in the boat then after returning her car to her driveway trotted back to the boat and pushed off from the float by five thirty.

Chapter 10

Bob didn't stumble back to the cabin until
well after dark. He was bone weary from
everything he had done the last couple of
days, but in spite of venting some of his
anger and frustration by packing in the
second side of deer he was feeling an
emotional drain. His verbal anger directed at
the girl had upset him, he realized that his
reaction had been out of character and he
was now feeling remorseful for his actions
and words.

After hanging up the second side of deer, he
stripped all his clothes off and washed his
whole body. The water was cold but still felt
good.

As he washed, his thoughts remained with
the girl, he kept seeing her face and her long
shock of black hair. He paused for a moment
as he recalled when she called him a
"bastard". In spite of himself he chuckled
and said aloud, "She's a feisty little devil
anyway. But I wonder where she got that
ridiculous idea that this island is hers."

After cleaning up he restarted the fire and
after going out and trimming off a piece of
deer fat he started to fry up some more liver,
then finding some withered mushrooms in
the vegetable box he added them to the
cooking meat.

Later, his belly full Bob pulled out his blankets from the pack sack and ignoring the blood splatters rolled into bed and immediately fell a sleep.

The next morning after a breakfast of fried venison, Bob skinned the second side and ruefully compared his job to what the girl had done. Next he cut some poles and erected a frame work over the fire pit. He then proceeded to cut the venison into strips and laid those across the poles. He started a fire and went into the bush and cut willows and alder and mixed the green wood in with the dry. He stood back and watched as the smoke drifted up and around the meat. Satisfied he continued cutting and dragging greenwood to the edge of the fire.

Once he thought, *'Wish I had some salt but I don't so smoke will have to do.'*

The air was reasonably cool so he had no worry about the rest of the meat spoiling for a couple of days and he figured that if he stoked up the fire at night with heavy wood the process would continue.

He took a break in the afternoon and went foraging for mushrooms and any berries that might still be about.

He found a patch of morels down by the water hole then up along the pines he gathered up a good quantity of pine mushrooms. He found a couple of bushes of blue huckleberries which were somewhat bitter but he picked them anyway. He knew he could get salal berries almost anytime so he avoided them.

He had luckily brought his water pails and pack sack so was able to get everything back in one load.

He stoked up the fire again then as there was still two or three hours of daylight left he trotted down to the beach and picked up a half dozen oysters.

As he started to head back to the trail, he turned and looked out over the water. There was nothing to be seen except the water, a jut of land several miles away and some seagulls wheeling over and diving into a probable school of small fish. Bob stared for several moments; for a moment a face framed in black hair crossed his mind but he shook his head, shrugged and turned again.

That night he feasted on venison heart, oysters and two types of mushrooms. *'Hmm you don't get 'surf and turf' better than this.'* He smiled in the darkness.

Later he stoked up the fire again, turned and moved the meat about then went to bed.

He awoke in the middle of the night to a roaring wind, the old cabin shook and the rain pounded like thunder on the shake roof. He went back to sleep but was awakened in the morning by the sound of dripping water.

Rain was leaking through the roof and falling on top of the stove. He put a bucket under the drip and went to check his meat. The fire was out, drowned by the torrential rain and one corner of his pole frame was skewed and several pieces of meat had fallen on the ground.

'Could be worse.' He thought.

He picked up the meat and took a tentative bite, "Hmm not bad although is it dry enough to keep?" He finished eating the strip then went and got some dry wood and restarted the fire.

Rain was still falling. Concerned that the rain would interfere with his curing process, Bob took the axe and cut several long poles then tying them together fashioned a rough tent frame.

He still had several pieces of plastic sheeting in the wood shed, these he draped over the frame and staked the edges outside of the pit. Immediately the smoke was compressed and some of the heat was trapped under the plastic. *'I should have thought of that sooner.'* He moved all the meat he had been curing to one end then added all that was left on to the cleared poles. As an after thought he closed off one end by fetching his travois and leaning it against one end. The smoke, although still escaping, was now relatively entrapped and no rain was falling on the meat or the fire.

Wind gusts still burst occasionally into the clearing so he tied and staked all the frame work even more securely.

Bob went back into the cabin and as the weather was still foul decided he would have an easy day and do some reading.

He had trouble focusing and his mind kept wandering to his visitor. *'I wonder where she went, will she really come back? This storm will tie her down and then she'll probably just move on.'*

He remembered her threat of bringing a gun and smiled. *'Ah, I just scared her, she won't be back.'*

He got up looked out the door, checking the smoking fire. He couldn't help staring at where the trail was for a few moments. He went back, sprawled on the bed and picked up his book again.

The following morning the rain had pretty well stopped but a gusty wind was still blowing. Bob hoisted himself up into the rafters and felt for the wet spot where the rain had dripped in. He couldn't detect a hole or a crack, but he measured with his hand how far from the chimney's edge the damp spot was then went outside.

He went around to the lean-to and rolled the chopping block to the lowest edge of the lean-to roof then clambered up and then onto the cabin roof. He didn't have to measure to locate the source of the problem. A knot in one of the shakes had cracked and shrunk. The water was seeping in and then running down on the next shake before dripping on to the stove.

He climbed back down intent on making a replacement shake when he remembered the pitch he had melted for the arrows.

He gathered up a few pieces and went inside to melt it down. By the time he got back outside and climbed back on the roof the pitch had congealed and wouldn't pour. "Shit." He muttered and sat back on his haunches to think.

A few moments later he was back on the ground. He put the pitch back on the stove. One of his water buckets was almost empty so he poured the remaining water into the other bucket then opened the door to the stove. He tipped the bucket and using a piece of kindling scraped embers into it. When the pitch was runny again he picked up the tin and put it into the bucket. A few minutes later he poured the pitch over the cracked knot and smoothed it with a stick. After checking the drying meat once more he gathered up his saw and the axe and headed down the trail to where he had noticed a dead standing hemlock. He spent the rest of the day, falling and bucking the tree into blocks. He managed to pack a third of the tree, one block at a time up to the lean-to. The remaining blocks he stacked saving them for another day.

Chapter 11

Bob slept until past daylight and as he slowly came awake he remembered the raft. 'Crap!" I better get over there." He said. Then thought, *'It should be all right, the storm came from my side of the island. But I better check'*

Deciding he would hurry, he slipped into his breech clout and moccasins, he picked up the empty water bucket, the axe and a coil of rope. He then checked the meat and deciding it was cured enough he grabbed a piece to chew on and headed out at a fast trot. In spite of the cool air brought in by the storm he was warmed by his exertions in the first few hundred yards and gradually broke into a light sweat.

At the pond he dropped the bucket as he ran past. A deer standing at the edge of the water watched him curiously as he sped by. He had just entered the forested part perhaps a quarter mile from the beach when he came across a tree that had undoubtedly been dislodged by the storm and lay at chest height across the path. It wasn't a large tree so he decided he would try and move it. In his haste he didn't notice that a larger tree had been blown over as well but was being held back by the branches of a third tree.

At chest level he knew he couldn't get a decent swing with the axe so he went down along the trunk to where he could climb up onto it. He walked along the trunk until he was over the path then jumped up and down. Inch by inch the tree settled downwards then stalled about two feet off the ground.

Bob jumped down and picking up the axe proceeded to chop the tree. With each swing a shock like wave went down the trunk and started a reaction by the transference of force fifty feet in the air. He was just lifting the axe to swing again when with a swishing noise the suspended tree slid down the branches that had restrained it and plummeted downwards. Too late Bob sensed something at the last moment and with the axe above his head he was crushed to the ground by the falling tree.

The side of the axe was driven against his head and one of the large limbs struck him on top of his head opening a deep gouge in his scalp.

Other branches scraped along his back and one side as he was smashed to the ground. Oblivion was instant.

Chapter 12

The sea was still choppy as Alicia crossed
the expanse of water. Even when she passed
by one of the many islands, the water
remained rough with waves reacting to tide
and hidden reefs and rocks.

It took slightly over two hours before she
slowed to make her approach to the beach.
But when she was a couple hundred yards
off shore she suddenly turned the outboard's
tiller and swung around and proceeded to go
around the island.

She increased her speed slightly and in a few
minutes passed the point where her
grandmother had beached her boat so long
ago and a few moments later and entered
into a channel. She could see rocks sticking
out of the water and some distance away
another island. She slowed and scanned the
beach looking for a landing spot that she
would feel comfortable about.

Finally she spotted a jumble of rocks with
what looked like drift logs caught along one
side. Beside the rocks and logs there was a
small stretch of pebbly beach interspersed
with patches of sand. She swung in slowing
the motor to an idle then as the motor's leg
bumped on the bottom, she killed the engine
and tilted the outboard.

The bow of the boat scraped and bumped along the beach and came to a halt.
Alicia jumped out onto the beach noticing that what she had thought to be just a bunch of drift logs was actually a raft and had obviously been secured to the rocks. She grabbed the bow and dragged the boat as far as she could, then took the bow rope and anchor and repeated the process that she had carried out a few days earlier on the other side of the island.

Knowing that she couldn't pack everything and actually now not sure exactly what her next step would be she pulled out her pack, the tube of papers and after a moments hesitation the wrapped rifle as well.

Finding the raft had suggested that there must be a trail nearby and after a searching for only a few moments found where Bob had dragged the deer and cut it into the two sides. It was then easy to find the start of the trail and she left the beach after one final look at her mooring line.

She was barely a hundred yards from the beach when she came to a couple of trees across the trail as she skirted around the tops she heard a strange sound and stopped. She stood for a moment listening but hearing nothing but a seagull's cry from out on the water and the chirping of a sparrow somewhere off in the bush, she shrugged and started to move on.

The noise came again, she cocked her head, listening. *'It's almost like a snore.'* She thought. She shrugged again and as she turned back to the deer trail she saw that a small branch from one of the fallen trees was quivering, the noise came again.

'Maybe a deer or something got hit and is trapped.'

She turned back towards the fallen tree and the quivering branch.

Alicia started to bend down to look closer when she spotted a bare leg sticking out from under the jumble of branches.

"Oh my God!" She cried.

She dropped to her knees and pulled some of the limbs away and saw part of Bob's near naked body being pinned to the ground. He was shivering violently. She started to call to him then realized she had never learned his name.

"Hey, hey, you can you hear me!" She called.

There was no response other than another stentorian snore like sound.

Alicia tugged frantically at the branches, breaking away some of the smaller ones but the larger ones she couldn't move.

She reached under the limbs thinking that maybe she could pull him out and her hand came in contact with the head of the axe. She pulled and worked it out from under his one arm and a large branch. As soon as it was free she attacked the outer limbs and worked her way to the tree trunk then in controlled swings cut away the entrapping limbs.

As soon as he was no longer ensnared she dropped the axe and fell to her knees. She started to try and roll him over then paused and starting at his shoulders felt the length of his body. She could detect no broken bones so she moved back up to his shoulders and with only a slight effort was able to roll him over. In doing so she found the deep gash on top of his head and the bruising high on the side of his face. Bob's mouth was open and every few seconds he emitted one of the snoring sounds. He continued to shiver violently.

Alicia jumped up and ran back around the fallen trees and back to her boat. She snatched up her rolled sleeping bag and the pup tent as well. She hurried back, laid the tent out on the ground then unrolled and opened her sleeping bag and spread it across the tent. She went to Bob's head and squatting down she got her hands under his arm pits and slowly straightened her legs.

She turned his body in a half circle and dragged him onto the sleeping bag then rolled it and the tent around him.

"Oh God he's so cold." She said aloud.

Chapter 13

Alicia squatted down beside Bob and tried to decide what she should next. She knew he was too cold and had no idea how long he had been lying on the ground. All his cuts and scrapes had stopped bleeding except for the one in his scalp and it was just oozing slowly. She thought of lighting a fire but rejected the idea as it came to her. He needed more than just a small camp fire. She didn't even consider trying to drag or trying to pack him. As she thought she suddenly remembered seeing a travois in the wood shed.

She tucked the clothes tightly around his body, pushed her pack tight up against him and propped the rifle against the fallen tree and took off on a run down the trail. She didn't attempt to run full out as she didn't know how far she had to go so settled into an easy pace. She came to and passed the water hole in about fifteen minutes and when she reached the fork she kept running up the slight incline without hesitation. She spotted the travois where it was now leaning against the smoking rack but continued by it and went into the cabin. Working as fast as she could, she kindled a fire in the stove and after adding some larger chunks of wood, she put some water on then hurried out the door, grabbed the travois and started back down the trail.

The round trip took over an hour and when she arrived back at Bob's side she found him still unconscious but thought that he wasn't shivering quite as much.

Realizing her body was warm and even sweaty from the run, she stripped down to her underclothing and un-tucking the sleeping bag slipped in beside him. She wrapped her arms and legs around him and pulled the sleeping bag tight around their bodies.

'Fifteen or twenty minutes then I've got to load him on and get going.' She thought. As she lay there she felt the shivering lessen even further, then realized that the snorting snores had quieted and he was breathing normally.

Alicia suddenly gave a small chuckle, *'Crap.'* She thought. *'I came here to evict him, maybe even shoot him and look at me now.'*

Finally she disentangled herself and slid out of the makeshift bed and hurriedly re-dressed herself.

As she positioned the travois she said "Well Mister Robert Anson or who ever you are, we have to get going. At least when you wake up I'll be in charge."

She pulled the sleeping bag off Bob and quickly dragged him onto the travois then recovered him again. She tucked the rifle, roll of papers and the axe in along side his body, slung her knap sack onto her back and bent down to heft the travois handles.

Alicia soon found the dead weight behind her was all she could handle. She realized quickly that she would have to have frequent rest breaks. It took her almost two hours to reach the pond where she rested for a long time; the final part up to the cabin was almost another two hours. By the time she stepped out into the clearing she was exhausted.

Alicia dragged the travois to the door, opened it and grabbed Bob under his shoulders and dragged him inside. She noticed immediately that he had returned to his earlier stupor and he was starting to shiver again.

She hoisted him half onto the bed then lifted and swung his legs up as well.

The cabin was still warm from the fire she had started earlier and after a moments hesitation, she opened the door to the stove and threw in a few pieces of kindling wood on the few embers that were left. She followed up with several larger pieces of wood as the kindling ignited.

She turned back to Bob and studied his prostrate form for a few seconds, she saw that in addition to his bruised head he had numerous scrapes, bruises and deep scratches. She started to look for a rag to clean the dirt and blood away, then realized that he may have more wounds so mentally shrugging she leaned over and rolled him over onto his back. His chest was dirty but there was no blood, his legs were the same. She hesitated once more then undid the leather sash that held his breechclout on. She paused again then shaking her head murmured aloud, "Don't be silly you have to check all over."

She pulled the breech clout off his hips and down over his feet. Blushing and angry with herself she examined all of his body then kneeling on the bed she rolled him on to one side and immediately found a puncture wound; a broken chunk of wood sticking out of the entry. Blood was slowly oozing from around the wood.

Her modesty and embarrassment immediately vanished and she rushed over to the stove and poured water, still hot from the fire she had lit earlier, into a bowl.

She looked around for something to use as a cloth, then pulled her shirt from out of her jeans and taking out her knife, cut then ripped away a piece of the material. She dipped the cloth in the bowl of water then washed all around the wound.

She sat on the edge of the bed and looked closely at puncture and the protruding wood. *'Its got to come out, but then the blood will really come.'* "Damn, I need a sponge or some gauze and something for disinfectant." She cried aloud, desperation in her voice. She jumped to her feet and went around the room, there was nothing. She dropped to her knees and peered under the bed and there was the survival kit Bob had found earlier. She dragged it out and dumped out the contents. The first aid kit was like a neon light! She grabbed it up and opened it. Inside was a small supply of gauze, a package of cotton batten, a bottle of iodine and a cardboard box of boric acid were the things that caught her eye.

She emptied and refilled the bowl with fresh water and poured almost half the bottle of iodine into the water. She looked for a second bowl but had to settle for a tin cup, into this she put a quantity of the boric acid and added water until she had a thin paste. She looked around the cabin again searching for something she could grip the broken branch with. When she couldn't find anything she said, "I guess that leaves my teeth and jaws."

She washed the wound with the iodine and water then carefully dried around the hole. She laid out a wad of cotton batten then after cutting a length of gauze and folding it into a pad, she knelt on the bed and bending down clenched her teeth over the protruding piece of wood.

Using her neck muscles she pulled upwards only to have her teeth slide off the tip of the wood. She wiped her mouth, bent down again and this time pushed her open mouth down around the stick pushing down into the flesh of Bob's buttock. She clenched her teeth again, but this time moved her head back and forth and side to side as she pulled. The stick slowly started to pull up out of the puncture then suddenly slid out with a sucking noise as Bob gave a mumbled sound of pain.

Blood immediately started to well up and out of the wound, Alicia spat the wood away and forced herself to wait a few seconds before trying to staunch the flow with cotton batten. For the first long minute it seemed that the blood was not going to stop. In seconds the cotton batten was a useless blood soaked mess. Alicia desperately pulled her blouse over her head and wadding it up pushed it against the wound and, pressed down.

Bob moved, although still unconscious he tried to roll away from the pain and the pressure.

"Lie still, damn you." Alicia cried her fear giving away to frustration and perhaps shock.

Bob's slight movement was all that his battered body could muster and he lay motionless again.

Time passed and Alicia finally relaxed the pressure then gently and carefully lifted the blood soaked blouse away. Blood still oozed but not gushing as before. Alicia remembered that she had guessed that there would be a large surge of blood and she relaxed slightly. She poured her boric acid mix over the wad of gauze and placed it over the wound.

She picked up the first aid kit and found a roll of tape tucked into one corner.

She dried all around the wound thoroughly then taped the gauze in place.

She sat back and stared at her handiwork for a few seconds then shook her head and said, "Can't rest yet, there's still work to be done."

She tore her blouse in two and rinsed out one half, then adding more water to the cup of boric acid paste she dipped a corner of what was left of her blouse into the thinned out paste and carefully cleaned all the other wounds and scratches. She wiped the bruise on the side of his head then parting his hair away from the gash on his head she cleaned down into the wound and around it with the iodine water. Knowing that she couldn't do anything more for the time being, she sat back then pulled a cover up over Bob, not quite sure if it was to keep him warm or just to cover him..

She slid off the bed went to the stove and poured the remaining water into the basin in one corner. She washed her hands and face, then looking down at her blood splattered chest, washed her whole upper body.

She found a shirt hanging from a nail, slipped it on and tied the tails around her waist.

'I wonder where that deer meat is.' Then remembering the frame over the fire pit she went out side and looked under the tent like structure over the fire pit.

'Well we're not going to starve.' She picked up a chunk and bit off a piece. Nodding her head she said, "Mm, not bad, But something has to be done with it."

She went back inside, checked Bob, who hadn't moved, then stoked up the stove and put on some more water noting that there was only a couple of inches left in the pail.

Chapter 14

Alicia sat and watched Bob for a few minutes then said aloud, "Well we'll need more water and I would think you'll sleep for awhile, 'sides there is something in those papers … but I can't remember what it is." She checked and added a piece of wood to the fire, picked up the pail and went out closing the door behind her. She jogged slowly for a bit then slowly picked up her pace into almost a run.

When she got to the pond she spotted the pail that Bob had dropped off early that morning, she tossed the other beside it and continued on along the path towards her boat.

Alicia skirted around the tree where she had found Bob and on to the beach. She checked her ropes once more then reached into the boat and picked up one of her boxes of supplies then headed back along the trail. Back at the pond she scooped one pail of water full and with it in one hand and the box under her other arm headed on to the cabin.

As she slowed to accommodate her load she started thinking about the tube of papers. Something was plucking at her memory, something about the cabin. Whatever it was stayed just beyond her mental grasp.

Her mind was still wrestling with the shadow memory as she once again entered the clearing.

She left the pail at the door and hurried in to check on her patient. He had shifted partly onto one side and was sleeping; his breathing sounded normal and feeling his forehead she decided that he may have a slight fever.

She moved away from the bed and put the box on the table then checked the fire once more.

She went out to where she had dropped the travois and picked up the tube of papers and went back inside.

She unscrewed the lid as she sat down on the chair then reached in and carefully pulled out the contents. She piled everything on the table then selected an old scribbler of the type that kids use to have in school, she thumbed quickly through the hand written pages, not finding what she was searching for she turned back to the first page and started again, reading and scanning as she turned the pages.

'I wish I had taken the time to read all of this more carefully before' she thought.
Finally she found what she was looking for, in her grandmother's neat school girlish handwriting were the words. "*Today we took up floor boards and started digging the cellar. Hard work*

and all the dirt has to be packed outside. " Several pages later there were another few lines. *"We finished the cellar at last now I can have a place to store my canning and some of the dried fish and stuff. Silas didn't want to do it but he is happy now that it is done. Moved the bed and now the cracks can't be seen.*

Alicia tossed the scribbler back on the table then turned and dropped to her hands and knees on the floor. She looked under the bed then felt with her hands, she immediately felt an evenness in the floor.

She stood up and checked Bob again then moving to the foot of the bed she pulled that end away from the wall then went around and pulled the head away as well. She repeated the exercise then knelt over the spot where the bed had been.

There was a three foot square area where the floor was obviously different and a quarter inch higher. There was a finger sized hole on the side next to the wall.

Without hesitating Alicia poked her middle finger in the hole, curled it and pulled upward. For a second nothing happened and she pulled harder and the square of wood gave and she lifted to reveal the opening in the floor.

She put the door to one side and kneeling felt around in the darkness below. She felt a

step a few inches down then reaching in
further, found a second step.

She jumped to her feet and went around to
the table and picked up a bottle holding a
candle. She lit it with one of the lighters and
went back to the hole. She set the bottle on
the floor, turned and lowered herself
backwards onto the steps below. When her
shoulders were level with the floor she
reached for the bottle and continued down
the ladder. She touched bottom just as the
top of her head was at floor level.

She held the candle at shoulder height and
turned to look about.

She sucked in her breath as she took in her
surroundings in the glow of the candle.

She was in a dirt walled room perhaps
twelve feet long and eight feet wide, just
smaller than the cabin. The cabin floor was
supported by a half dozen of six inch cedar
posts. A dirt shelf had been dug along one of
the long sides with a second shelf resting on
it made of split logs.

Along the other long wall and one end wall
were three more shelves made from more of
the split logs.

On the other end a beam ran between two of
the posts, several shriveled objects hung
from the beam.

But what really caught her eye was the dozens of jars, obviously full stacked on several of the shelves.

One shelf at the foot of the ladder held several more dozen empty jars and cardboard boxes which turned out to be canning lids.

Alicia walked slowly around the shelves, finally she took down a quart sealer that was obviously salmon, another pint sealer of what she thought may be berries and another quart sealer of carrots. She carried these to the foot of the ladder, blew out the candle and in two trips had everything up the ladder and on the floor.

She replaced the trap door and as she started to move the bed back, she stopped, then after pacing out its length decided she could move it under the one window and leave the trap door accessible. It fit with inches to spare.

Alicia felt Bob's forehead and then his chest area. Nodding her head, satisfied that his temperature hadn't risen she took the three jars to the table and checked the lids. They were tightly sealed, not bulged and after wiping off the dust she could see that each jar's contents appeared to be unblemished.

Feeling a pang of hunger, Alicia glanced at her watch, *'five fifteen, the day is almost over, no wonder I'm hungry'* she thought.

She poked the fire into activity, half filled a pot with water and put it on the stove then went out side. She returned in a moment with a chunk of the smoked meat and dropped it into the pot.

She turned her attention back to the jars then taking a small paring knife from the table drawer, she punctured the lid on the jar of salmon and pried it off.

Cautiously she sniffed the contents and licking her lips she said aloud, "smells damn fine."

She sat down on the chair and drumming her fingers on the table stared at the jar of salmon. "Well I've got no way to test it, there's no reason it should be bad so…."

She grabbed a fork from the drawer and picked off a finger nail sized piece of the fish and with out any more hesitation popped it in her mouth, chewed and swallowed.

Next she opened the carrots and ate a piece of one then followed suit with the last jar which actually turned out to be salal berries. She ate the several of those and drank some of the juice.

She turned her attention back to Bob, "You Mr. Trespasser will get broth until we see how my body stomachs the canning."

Chapter 15

Still hungry, Alicia cut away a piece of the
deer meat in the pot and sat down as she
chewed on it.

*'I wonder if I should wake him up, he needs
food as well, but sleeping is good too.'*

Leaving the water in the pot to boil, she
fished out the remaining chunk of meat and
carrying it to the table she painstakingly cut
it up in to tiny pieces then dumped it back
into the now boiling water.

"I'll give it a half hour then after it's cool
I'll wake you up." She said to Bob's still
form.

She watched him for a moment then went to
the end of the bed and kneeling lifted the
trap door again. She relit the candle and
lowered herself once more into the chamber.
She picked up one of the cartons of lids,
climbed the ladder and shoved the carton out
onto the floor. She backed down the stairs
again and walked to the shelves where the
empty bottles were boxed, not trusting the
cardboard box they were stored in she
carried them six at a time to the ladder then
after she had two dozen she moved them up
and onto the floor a few at a time.

When the last two dozen were up she blew out the candle and hoisted herself out of the hole.

She reset the door then moved around the cabin looking for something, anything that she could boil a large quantity of water in. The only thing of any size were the two pails used for carrying water.

"C'mon, there must be something, Grandma didn't preserve all that stuff in a small pot. She went outside and around to the woodshed, there was nothing there. As she went back around to the door she shivered in the evening air, then realized she had no blouse and her upper body was clad only in a brassiere. Instinctively she wrapped her arms around her body with the realization, then chuckled as she remembered she had been relatively unclothed for the last few hours not to mention when she had climbed into the sleeping bag earlier in the day almost totally nude.

Back inside she took a shirt that was hanging on a nail and slipped it on. It was much too big so she tied the tails into a knot. Her mind returned to the need for a kettle of some sort then a thought struck her.

Once more she lit the candle, lifted the trap door and went down the steps.

She walked slowly around the room and as she came full circle to the ladder she saw something behind the ladder and up on the dirt bank. It was an old copper boiler oblong in shape with a handle on each end. A lid was sticking out of the top. "Yes!" she cried. She pulled it off its perch and pushed it up the steps ahead of herself. Blew out the candle and again replaced the door.

Alicia set to work cleaning the old boiler and was quite relieved to find it had no holes or rust spots at the seams. After it was cleaned to her satisfaction she put it on the stove and added three or four inches of water. While she waited for that water to boil she selected two dozen of the quart sealers and washed and dried them as well then put them upside down into the heating water.

Next she went out and carried back in several pot loads of the smoked meat, she cut it into smaller chunks, trimmed off much of the fat and piled it all to one side.

After rewashing the pot she had carried the meat in she filled it with water and added a several table spoons of salt and put the pot on the remaining corner of the stove.

By the time she had finished this preparation the boiler of jars had come to the boil but she left them a bit longer and took a break from her labour to check her patient.

Bob's fever had lessened to the point that she wasn't sure if he still had one.

Alicia poured some of the meat particle broth she had made earlier into a large mug and sat down on the edge of the bed.

"Hey, hey you. Can you hear me?" She asked.

Bob didn't move so she reached out and gently patted his one exposed shoulder.

"Hey, c'mon wake up it's supper time."

Bob moved a bit and his eyelids twitched, she shook his shoulder and repeated her words.

Bob groaned quietly, his eyelids fluttered then he opened his eyes. He stared straight ahead for a few seconds, his eyes unfocused, then he blinked a couple of times and turned his head slowly becoming aware and as it registered in his mind that Alicia was leaning over him, he blinked again and started to speak. His mouth was too dry and the couple of words were more like a croak. Alicia realized what the problem was and putting the mug on the table she rushed over and dipped another cup into the one water pail that had water and took it back to the bed.

She again sat on the bed but had to slide over so she could support his head while he sipped the water.

As he sipped and swallowed Alicia said "Welcome back, you have a few bumps and contusions plus a nasty hole in your uh er ah hip area."

Bob moved his head away from the cup and asked, "What happened? How did I get here and what are you doing here?"

"Never mind right now, here I have some meat broth. Drink it up and I can give you some more."

Alicia put the water cup down and picked up the cup of broth.

Bob struggled to sit up, winced in pain and drew in a sharp breath as he stretched and pulled his buttock area.

"Stop, stop," Alicia cried. "You'll open the wound or at least tear off your bandage. I'll prop you up while you drink it."

Bob acquiesced and sipped then gulped the broth as he tasted it and his hunger came to life.

He drank it all and Alicia asked if he wanted more.

"No, uh no thanks, maybe in a little while. Uh it was good thank you."

Alicia lowered his head then tucked the second pillow under his head. "I've got a project started here, I'll work at that and when you're ready I tell you as much as I can about what happened."

She turned back to the stove and lifted the boiler off and set it on the floor. After washing her hands she gingerly lifted the

jars out of the water and set them in rows on
the table then started cramming each jar
with the cut up venison. When she was
finished she poured equal quantities of the
salted water into each of the jars. As she
finished she looked down at the packages of
lids and under her breath said, "Damn not
enough lids." She swished out the salt water
pot and poured in a couple of inches of
water and put it back on the stove. "Double
damn," she muttered a little louder, "I need
the screw rings."

Bob had been watching her activities and
finally asked "Where'd you find those jars?"

"Right under your bed where I am going
right now." She replied.

Bob frowned but remained silent as she
went around the bed, lifted the trap door and
taking her candle disappeared from his view.
He opened his mouth to call out then closed
it as he waited for to reappear.

In a couple of minutes she was back up with
a wooden box full of sealer rings and two
more sealed and dusty jars.

Bob stared in amazement, "You mean
there's a door and a room under the floor"?
He asked.

Alicia nodded, "Yep and a bunch of canning
and preserves. Which reminds me that there
has been no repercussions from what I ate
earlier."

As she set her load down on the edge of the table she said, "By the way what's your name? I can't just be calling you, hey you." He stared at her for a second then said, "It's Bob, what's yours?"

"My name is Alicia and you may as well know now that hurt or not you have been trespassing on my property Mr. Bob, missing from Hubbard Island Anson and when I get you well enough you will be leaving."

Bob's jaw dropped, "How, how did you find out about me?"

"Your description and a picture is posted up at the RCMP office, I must say the picture looks better than you do. Your brother is looking for you."

As they talked Alicia drooped the lids and the rings into the boiling water , waited a few minute then and started extracting and placing the lids on the waiting jars.

Bob started to say something more then lapsed into silence and quietly watched Alicia work.

She put the large boiler back on the stove. When all the lids were in place she fished out the rings and screwed them down over the lids on each jar.

Once the boiler was at the boil again she added all the jars one by one, there was no room for two of them so she put them into

the pot she had sterilized the lids and rings
in.

Without saying a word Alicia went out side
and returned in a few moments with a
weathered piece of plywood which she put
across the top of the boiler.

She checked her watch and muttered
"Already quarter after five about eight
fifteen then."

Chapter 16

Her labours finished for the moment, Alicia put a small helping of fish and carrots on a plate from the two opened jars, she turned to Bob and asked, "Want some more broth? I don't think you should have any of this as I'm still testing it."

Bob nodded, "Yes that would be nice, thanks. Is there still more of the venison?"

"Not very much, by the time I finished deboning it most of it fit in the jars." Alicia poured another cup of the broth and set it on the table. "You look a lot stronger, I'll help you sit up and see if you can manage on your own."

A moment later, Bob all propped up started to sip the broth then paused. "Uh, Alicia, uh you know my name, I guess I should know all of yours."

Alicia smiled and replied, "Of course, it's Alicia, Alicia Aleuta Ferguson Davis. Bob took a couple more sips of the broth, watching Alicia as she started to eat.

Lowering the cup from his lips, Bob cleared his throat and said, "I'm sorry about the row we had, you said that this cabin and everything is yours?"

Nodding, Alicia chewed and swallowed her mouthful of food, "Yes, it is the island as well. I've brought the papers that prove it. Do you want to see them now?"

"Oh no, not right now. Finish eating and you can show me later." Bob sipped again at his cup.

They both sat in silence as Alicia finished her meal and Bob his broth. The only noise for the next few minutes was the occasional popping sound of burning wood in the barrel stove.

Alicia pushed her plate back and asked, "How do you feel? Do you want to lie back again?"

"No, I'm okay thanks, best if I sit up and gain some energy back."

"Well sitting up will probably do the reverse, but you have slept all day so a little longer won't hurt you."

Alicia checked the boiler and then opened the stove door and put the last stick of wood on the fire. "I have to bring in some more wood, be right back."

The moment she was out the door, Bob lifted the covers and confirmed that he was naked, he felt along his backside and found the bandage on his buttock, *'Jesus, she has been a busy gal, but how'd she get me here?'*

Alicia brought in three arm loads of wood and stacked them in the wood box. She turned to Bob and asked, "By the way where's your toilet, I can't keep running off into the bush."

Bob waved his arm towards one corner of the building, "Out here on past the garden, about twenty or thirty yards into the bush. Actually it's just a "Johnson bar" over a hole in the ground."

Alicia smiled, "I know about those. Thanks, I'll be right back." She went back out the door into the dusk.

As soon as the door closed Bob hitched himself painfully to the edge of the bed then carefully swung his legs over the edge. Sweat formed in large drops on his forehead as pain radiated from all the bruised areas and the wound in his buttock. He struggled to his feet and tried to take a step but then slumped back onto the bed with a small groan. "Damn," he whispered, "I've really got to go."

He rested a second and then as he pushed himself upright once more the door swung open and Alicia stepped inside.

"What are you doing? Get back on that bed." She cried.

Bob pulled the sheet around himself and glaring at her said, "You're not the only one around here that needs to go you know."

Alicia instantly looked contrite, "Oh Bob, I am sorry. I should have asked, I never thought."

"Okay. That's okay, but there is a big can over there in the corner, would you get it for me please?"

Alicia found the tin and passed it to Bob, "I'll wait outside, call me when you're finished." She hurried back through the door.

A minute later Bob called, "Okay you can come back."

Alicia entered and crossed the room and took the tin from Bob and put it on the floor. "Here I'll help you get comfortable again." Bob started to protest then nodded and eased back onto the edge of the bed.

Alicia bent and grabbing his heels swung him slowly and gently around then as Bob propped himself on his arms, she moved the two pillows behind his back and helped him to sit back in a half reclining position.

"From now on let me know what you need." Alicia said.

Bob nodded, "Okay, but by tomorrow I should be able to move around."

"Maybe, we'll see," was the reply, "but now I better have a look at your backside and see if the bandage is okay."

Bob opened his mouth to protest then shrugging slightly turned over to his undamaged side.

Alicia pulled the sheet aside and lifted one corner of the bandage, "Looks okay but since we're this far, I think I'll wash the area and put on a fresh bandage."

She poured some water, washed her hands and mixed up some more boric acid solution. Ten minutes later a fresh bandage was in place.

As Bob rolled onto his back he said, "Uh I think there's some under shorts over there in that box," he gestured towards the end wall, "maybe I should put them on."

Alicia, without a word walked over, got the shorts and gave them to him then turned and busied herself with putting more wood in the fire and burning the old bandage.

Bob struggled into the under shorts and as he settled himself he said, "I guess we better talk about the cabin and the island. You knew about the cellar so I guess that means you have some knowledge about the place which supports what you said the other day."

Alicia turned from the stove and said, "Look we don't have to talk about that right now. It can wait until tomorrow or the next day."

"No, let's have it now, we have nothing else to do while the meat is cooking."

Alicia shrugged and said, "Okay, suit your self, I've brought copies of everything and you can read it all for yourself."

She fished out the rest of the papers from the canister and carrying them over to the bed she laid them beside him.

"There it all is, I am the granddaughter of Marcet." She turned away and busied herself with getting more wood and cleaning up the table and putting things away.

Bob quickly scanned through the papers then started over and read through them all carefully. He knew from the first scan that Alicia's claim was bona fide, but his curiosity was aroused and he found the documents historically interesting.

Finally finished, he carefully set the papers to one side and watched Alicia as she puttered about.

Feeling his gaze Alicia straightened up from storing the utensils and turned to look back, a questioning g look on her face.

There eyes held for a moment then Bob said, "First I owe you an apology, obviously this, everything is yours and not only am I trespassing but I guess I was rude the last time, I'm sorry I'm not usually like that."

Alicia stared at the window for a moment then replied, "Look, you were a castaway, and it was only chance that brought you here and I must say you have made things look pretty good. And I guess I was a bit mouthy as well." She smiled then gave a small chuckle, "Let's start all over."

He smiled back, "I'd like that and I also have to thank you for, I am sure, saving my life."

Alicia didn't say anything in reply but smiled and got up to light a candle.

They both fell silent for a few moments, then Alicia said, "Okay let's get to know a bit about each other, all I know about you is that you are missing and you ended up here."

Bob hesitated then giving in to a hidden need he launched into telling the tragedy that had caused him to go into seclusion and on to the storm and finding himself on the island. In the flickering candle light, Alicia had moved over and sat on the edge of the bed as he started; when he told about the loss of his wife she reached out and squeezed his hand, his fingers automatically closed over hers and their hands remained clasped until he arrived at his first stirring after waking up on the island.

By the time Bob was finished it was after eight o'clock, Alicia rose and checked the jars then using a large spoon and a dish rag carefully lifted all the jars out of the water and placed them on the table.

"I'll leave the boiler on the stove as I don't want to be spilling that boiling water." She replaced her makeshift lid. She had hardly

turned from the stove when the first jar
made a tinkling pop as the lid sealed itself.
Bob squirmed gingerly about, finding a
more comfortable position then said, "Now
it's your turn, let's hear all about you."
"I don't know, are you sure you're not too
tired? Alicia asked.
"Not at all, I think I must have slept most of
the day as it is."
"Okay, if you are sure, but I think I have to
start back with my Grandmother and work
my way forward."
"Sure thing, go ahead."
Accompanied by the sound of popping lids,
Alicia told the story of how her grandmother
had met her grandfather; just after she
started she paused as it suddenly struck her
how similar that meeting had been to hers
and Bob's situation. When she stopped Bob
looked at her with raised eyebrows but she
just shook her head and moved on.
As she talked, Bob's eyes started to droop
and by the time she started to relate her
parents story he had fallen sound asleep.
Alicia quit talking as soon as she noticed
that Bob had dozed off and instead started
humming a tune as she rose and checked the
jars.
Stretching and yawning she glanced about
and suddenly realized that she had a choice

between the floor or a narrow piece of the bed as a place to sleep.

She gathered together the assorted clothes that were hanging about and made a makeshift mattress on the floor.

She had a quick wash in the basin then pulling off her boots she knelt down and stretched out on the thin pile of clothes. The cabin was warm and exhausted by the day's events she fell asleep in minutes.

Chapter 17

Sometime, in the middle of the night, Alicia awoke, she was cold and curled up lying mostly on the hard wooden floor.

She rearranged the clothes and lay down again but now that the cabin had cooled down she couldn't get warm. She squirmed and wriggled about but the hard floor and the cold room gave her no respite.

Finally she muttered, "Oh to hell with it, I need to get some sleep."

She stood up, pulled on a jacket from what had been her mattress and gingerly sat then stretched out on the bed at Bob's side.

She cautiously rolled over facing away from him and closed her eyes.

Sleep was elusive for only a few minutes.

Alicia was awakened by Bob trying to get out of the far side of the bed.

"What are you doing, where are you…?"

Bob cut her off, "Gotta go. I need the can."

Alicia started to make a sharp retort then realizing that what had to be had to be said, "Just wait I'll get it for you."

She got up found the can and passed it across the bed, "Me too I guess, I'll be right back."

She slipped on her boots and went out through the door.

When she got back she found Bob standing up the can in one hand and the other clutching the headstead.

"Don't be silly." She cried. "I can take care of that. Here give it to me."

Bob passed over the can and carefully sat down on the bed. "Thanks, I thought maybe I could make it to the door but I'm too stiff."

"Well layback and roll over and I'll have a look at the hole and redress it."

Bob did as he was told. Alicia washed her hands then pulled down the top of his shorts and slowly removed the bandage.

Pleased with what she saw she said, "Good it has good color and a scab has started to form." She fetched the bowl of boric acid water and washed all around the wound, waited until it had air dried then painted around the outside with more iodine. She put a light gauze bandage over it and taped the bandage in place. "There." She said, "That should be good until tonight, now how about some breakfast?"

"Uh yeah, I guess but I got another problem," Bob replied.

"What?"

"Uh I need to go out side to, to well you know."

Alicia stared at him, "I don't see how that will work. Can't you use the can?"

145

"No, absolutely not." Was the forceful answer, then, "Perhaps if I leaned on you, you could help me get there."

Alicia cocked her head, thought for a moment then said, "Okay let's give it a try." Twenty minutes later, Bob, his face pale, stood in front of the 'johnson bar' and said "Okay, I can manage now."

Alicia bit her lip then saying nothing turned and walked away. When she was out of sight she called back, "I'll wait right out here!"

A few minutes went by then Bob called, "Okay, you can come back."

Standing there in the bushes clad only in a pair of underwear and gum boots Bob was rather a ludicrous site. Alicia forced herself not to show any levity and once again got one of his arms across her shoulders and together they made their way back.

When they got to the door, Alicia said, "After breakfast I'll try and find something for a crutch."

Bob just grunted, still embarrassed by the whole episode.

Back inside, Bob lay back on the bed while Alicia bustled about rekindling the fire and putting water on to heat. "This is the last of the water, so I'll have to get some a bit later." she said.

A short while later after a breakfast of canned berries and a whole jar of canned salmon between them, Alicia put the tin Bob had been using as a commode beside the bed and said, "I'll just head out and see what I can find for a crutch, be back in a few minutes."

"Okay," Bob said. But could you toss me over that pocket book and maybe I could look at your papers again?"

Alicia did as asked and went and around to the shed at the back. She couldn't find anything suitable for what she wanted so picked up the axe and struck off down the trail that led to where the signal fire had been set.

She noted that it had obviously been repiled with fresh wood in the recent past. *'Looks like he had intended to leave at some point.'* She thought. She circled around the half clearing and then struck off into the surrounding bush. She walked slowly looking mostly at small trees. Finally she spotted what she had been searching for, a small tree two or three inches thick that was forked over six feet above the ground.

She quickly chopped it down, cutting at ground level, then cut the two forks leaving a 'y' shaped piece of wood. She trimmed off the few small branches that were left then axe in one hand and the tree in the other she retraced her steps back to the cabin.

Chapter 18

Back at the cabin, Alicia had Bob stand up and together they figured out how long the shaft of what was going to be a crutch should be and she cut it off to that length. "There that should help you have some independence," she said. "I'll let you trim it up or whatever you need to do to make it comfortable."

"Sure, there's a leatherman in one of my pants, it has a good blade on it and I can whittle it down."

Alicia, after a brief search, found the knife and brought it to Bob. "I'm going to use the few meat scraps that are left and some of the bones from your deer and make us a stew for supper while you're working on that."

They both turned to their tasks and after a little while Bob said, "Alicia can you hang here for a couple of days until this thing of mine heals? And then can I get a ride into Ucluelet with you?"

"Well of course I'll stay, I can't very well leave you like this."

"Thanks," he replied, "and you didn't finish your story last night."

She laughed, "Well it must be pretty boring, you fell asleep while I was talking."

He laughed as well, "Guess you're right, well I'm awake now."

Alicia , thought for a moment, then picking up from just before she had noticed that he had dropped off, she continued with the rest of her story.

After a short while Bob stopped whittling and watched her as she talked. He saw the emotions that she couldn't conceal and in his mind joined her almost in a visual way as she related the story up to her arrival and their earlier confrontation.

Eventually she finished talking and the small room was silent. Bob was still staring at her and after a few seconds she turned to look at him and their eyes locked and held for many seconds more. Finally, as though by some unspoken agreement they both looked away and continued with their chores.

"After a little while Bob said, "You didn't say if I can catch a ride with you."

"Oh, oh that of course, but you can stay on here for awhile if you want."

"Thanks, but no, I better let my brother know and get on with becoming un-hermitized."

Alicia nodded, "Yes I guess that is a good idea and I am sure there must be some legal ramifications that may have to be dealt with as a result of your being missing. Right now though I'm going to leave you on your own for an hour or more. We need water and I still have a couple of things in the boat." She paused, "No forget that stuff for today. I just remembered my sleeping bag and tent are on that travois thing, I'll bring them in and make sure they're dry and tonight I'll be able to put the whole night in on the floor." She jumped up and brought in the two forgotten items and after a short struggle got them both hanging from the rafters. "Now, I'm off for that water." She picked up the two pails and was gone.

Bob lay back on the bed for a few minutes then shaking his head slightly he said to the empty room, "Sure was a lot better when she was here talking." He smiled to himself. He whittled on the rough crutch until he was satisfied then struggled up off the bed and onto his feet. For the first few steps around the room he was awkward and almost fell once. Then getting the hang of it he made several circuits, getting better each time he completed a lap.

He managed to get the stove door open and tossed in a stick of wood, then closed the door again.

He sat and rested for a few minutes then decided to go out to his bush toilet. He made that short trip easily although he caught one foot on a protruding root and almost fell. Back in the cabin, he stretched out on the bed and lay back; his mind galloped through

the events of the last few months, slipping
back briefly to when his wife had died. Then
relived what he could remember of the boat
sinking, he recalled the confrontation with
Alicia and walked slowly through the last
two days and how she had undoubtedly
saved his life.

He dozed off only to be awoken by Alicia as
she banged through the door and deposited
the pails on the floor.

"I think I'll fill a few pots and whatever else
you have and go get another pail, then we
should be good for a couple days." She
announced.

A few minutes later she was gone out the
door once more.

Bob sat up as she left and stared at the table
laden with the canning of the night before.

*'We don't need all that for awhile so I better
do something.'* He thought.

He got to his feet then crutch under one arm
he laboriously relocated the jars two at a
time to the edge of the trap door. He found
the bending down to place each pair of jars
the hardest part but kept at it until only a
half dozen jars remained on the table. These
he moved to a rough shelf along one wall.
Restricted by the injury and finding nothing
more to do, he hobbled out into the yard and
looked around the clearing. The fire pit and

its ramshackle smoking shelter struck him as something he could work at.

Supported by the crutch he managed with his one arm to pull everything down and away then piled the poles reasonably neatly then dragged the plastic around to the shed. There he sat down on the chopping block and folded the plastic into a bundle.

As he was finishing he heard Alicia call his name, "Bob! Bob where are you. Bob?" Rather than answer he decide to just walk back around the cabin when he heard her call even more loudly, "Bob, Bob! Where the hell are you?"

As he rounded the cabin he saw Alicia standing just out side the door, a frightened look on her face. "I'm here, right here." She whirled around, "Don't do that, I was scared you'd fallen or something. Why didn't you answer?"

Bob shrugged then realizing that she had been scared mumbled, "Sorry, didn't mean to upset you, I've just been puttering about." Alicia glared at him for a couple of seconds then her features softened and she replied, "I'm sorry too, I guess I let my imagination take over. I see you've been working, I hope you're not overdoing it."

"Nah, I'm fine and I think the exercise is helping loosen things up."

They both went inside, Alicia immediately saw that the jars had been moved, as she turned to ask, Bob said, "Over there, on the floor, you'll have to take them below." Alicia nodded, then said, "Okay but first I'm going to clean up this place a bit then I'll take them down. You better have a rest." As Alicia, cleaned the cabin, they chatted back and forth, each without realizing were seeing inside each other and also without realizing were form a bond from the exchange of stories, ideas and feelings.

Chapter 19

The next day passed uneventfully, they continued with getting acquainted. Spasmodic sunshine encouraged them to spend sometime outside and leaning back against the building they sat for over an hour, not speaking, each lost in their own thoughts. Before they went to bed that night Alicia examined all Bob's scrapes, cuts and the large wound. Most of the minor wounds had already disappeared or were small reddish scars; the puncture had healed well with a well formed scab encircled by a red ring. She washed it once more with a boric acid solution and put a small bandage on to protect the scab. "It'll be just fine," she pronounced. "Keep that on for a couple of days and you should be as good as new." The day following after breakfast Bob said, "I hardly used the crutch at all yesterday afternoon, how about going for a walk to the beach?"

"Sure thing but we should take the thing along in case you need it at some point."

"Nah, I won't need it I'm really feeling pretty good."

Alicia stared at him for a moment, then said "Okay let's go, you lead off."

As Bob limped off down the trail, she scooped up the crutch and swung it on to her shoulder and followed along.

When they got to the fork, Bob hesitated and Alicia said, "Let's go to the closer one, if you are okay with that we can go to the other tomorrow or the next day."

Looking back Bob nodded, his eyes widened when he saw the crutch, he started to say something, thought better of it and moved on along the trail.

When they got to the beach they sat on a log for a few minutes and gazed out over the water.

Then Bob turned to Alicia, "Say, how about some fresh fish?"

"Good idea," she replied. "How do we get some?"

"I have a rod and some tackle stashed over there," he waved his arm down the beach. "I guess it actually belongs to you."

They started along the beach, Bob moving more slowly among the rocks and gravel, they arrived at the hiding spot and Bob said, "Wait here and I'll go get a couple."

"No Bob, I think you should let me, once in the water you could catch your foot and pull that wound open."

"Yeah but the salt water should be good for it."

"Then you can sit in the water and soak it while I use my rod to get the fish."

Bob glared at her for a second then started to grin, "God you're a bossy woman, but yeah I guess you're right."

Alicia started towards the water then stopped. "Turn your head, I have to take off my jeans."

Bob looked at her, colored a bit and mumbled, "Oh, yeah sure." He turned his back to the water.

A few minutes later Alicia called, "Okay! And seriously why don't you sit in the water And splash some over the wound?"

"I think I will," he called back, "tend to your fishing."

While Alicia made her first cast he pulled off his pants and hobbled down to the water, he waded out to just below his knees and sat down.

The first fish Alicia caught was a small rock fish, she started to throw it back then changed her mind and set the treble hook into the flesh along the upper back then flung the baited lure outward to land about twenty feet away.

She stood and waited while the small fish tugged away at the line and after a few minutes reeled it back in.

She peeled off about thirty feet of line into the water, then grabbing the fish's lower jaw between thumb and fore finger flung it back out in a slightly different direction. The fish went almost the full thirty feet before it landed again in the water.

Again she waited patiently then she felt a small jerk that was subtly different than what the rock fish had been doing, a second later there was a tremendous tug and the rod bent sharply, line screamed from the reel! Bob jerked straight up to the sound, "Hey you got a good one on."

Alicia didn't reply, she was intent on tightening the drag without over doing it. Slowly she slowed the run and as the unseen fish turned and swam towards her she frantically recaptured the line that had been stripped off and tried to retain tension between her and the fish.

After a couple of moments the fish attempted to regain some dominance by going from one side to the other, swimming back towards Alicia tugging away and just using its weight.

All of this was countered by Alicia as she expertly played the fish and wore it down. Finally after what seemed like an eternity but was actually less than fifteen minutes she had it within a few feet of where she was standing. With the fish fairly docile she slowly backed towards shore and intent on the job at hand she totally forgot that she was clad only in her panties below her waist. Bob, intent on her struggle, didn't at first notice her near nakedness then his attention shifted from where the line swished in the water to Alicia herself then down to her water revealed hips and buttocks.

He stared open mouth, the fish momentarily forgotten.

Alicia turned to shout an instruction and caught him staring.

She glanced down and realized that her water soaked panties left little to the imagination. "Never mind your gawking, get ready to help while I get this thing into the shallows, he may have another run left."

Bob struggled to his feet his face flushed from the embarrassment of being caught staring. He started to move back then decided that he was probably in as good a spot as any to help, he waited as Alicia slowly backed towards him, he stared fixedly at the spot where the line entered the water.

Alicia drew abreast of Bob and slowly continued backing towards the shore, she swung the rod tip so that the line came very close to Bob's legs.

"Okay, I think I see him, it's a big ling," Bob said. "Stop when I say and I'll get a hand into his gill."

A few seconds later, "Okay stop but keep the line tight."

The fish was right at Bobs feet, lying partly on its side. He bent down and slowly put one hand below the water but the moment he touched the fish it gave another twisting lunge to one side.

Alicia raised the rod tip higher and kept tension on the line.

The fish fought for a few seconds but got feebler with each twist then suddenly gave up and rolled completely onto one side.

Bob quickly slipped his hand inside the gill cover and as quickly lifted the fish out of the water and turned towards shore. He walked out onto the beach and carefully disengaged his hand from the gills, then picked up a stick of drift wood and clubbed the ling cod across the head.

"Bet it runs about twenty pounds, nice work Alicia."

When she didn't respond Bob looked up to see her staring fixedly down the beach, "What's wrong, what do you see?" He asked.

"Nothing, just go get your pants on," was the reply.

"What?" He started and then looking down realized that his wet shorts were no more less revealing than her wet underwear was.

He hobbled over to his pants and while he pulled his jeans on Alicia redressed herself. Neither said any thing until they were fully dressed, then Bob said, "Here, I'll gut this thing out, no, I'll filet it and we can leave everything here for the crabs."

Alicia, now composed walked over and looked at her catch, "I think it's big enough to do the cheeks as well."

Bob looked down at the head, "You're right, we can have them as a snack when we get up to the cabin."

Alicia wound the line all in, and put the rod back in its hiding place while Bob filleted the fish.

A few minutes later they were on their way back up the trail. Bob using the crutch.

They had just left the beach when Alicia said, "Wait, I forgot something, you go ahead I'll catch up."

She turned without waiting for an answer and ran back to the beach.

She hurried along the waters edge for a few feet then finding what she was looking for, she started picking up one type of seaweed that had been left at the tide line she carried it all after making the front of her shirt into a sack. She then turned and hurried back catching up with Bob just a few yards from the cabin's clearing.

Chapter 20

The morning had passed quickly and by the time they got back to the cabin it was lunch time.

Bob rekindled the fire while Alicia skinned the two cheeks and cut and washed to small pieces from one of the fillets.

She then washed the remaining fish and said, "Bob, Have you got anywhere reasonably cool to keep these?"

He said, "Actually I have, I made a sort of root cellar on the south side over there, for the potatoes and carrots."

"What potatoes and carrots?"

"Oh I guess I forgot, I did get a bit of a harvest and I stored them in it. Sorry I just plumb forgot."

Alicia smiled instantly, "Of course you forgot, you've had a bit more on your mind with other things when your mind has been awake."

"How about putting the fish in it and bringing back a couple of spuds?"

Bob nodded, picked up the fish and went out the door.

They fried fish and sliced potatoes in deer tallow, they chatted back and forth as they ate, but periodically there were short silences during which they both felt inexplicable embarrassment.

Later after the dishes had been washed and put away, Bob cleared his throat and said, "I've been thinking; my butt is doing fine and I'm sure you want to get back, so whenever you are ready I'm ready."

Alicia studied him for a moment then said, "Okay let's leave in the morning, I can bring the boat around to this side and pick you up."

Bob shook his head, "No I wouldn't mind doing the walk a cross and going by the water hole." He smiled slightly, "Sort of a last walk for the sake of nostalgia."

Alicia nodded, "Sure thing, I understand."

They sat for a bit saying little the Bob stood up, "Hey do you like to play cards? There's an old deck here somewhere."

"Yes I do, do you play crib?"

Bob found the deck after a brief search and they whiled away the afternoon playing cards.

At one point Alicia exclaimed, "Oh damn, I was going to make flour then Indian bread with that sea weed, if we're leaving tomorrow I won't be able to."

Bob said, "That's okay you can make it for us another time." He paused briefly, embarrassed by what he had implied, he hurried on, "The garden we can spread it on the garden."

If Alicia had caught his slip she gave no outward sign.

They continued playing cards and while they did, rain started to spatter on the roof then after a while turned into a solid down pour.

Alicia went to the door and looked out, "It'll be wet trip if this keeps up."

"Well we can always leave a bit later, it would be nice to be reasonably dry when we get to your boat."

"True." Alicia said, "And if a storm comes up we'll just wait it out, we don't have to leave."

For dinner they finished the one slab of ling cod that Alicia steamed in a mixture onions and chopped carrots.

"Where did you learn to do that?" Bob asked as he swallowed his last bite and wiped his lips.

"Well to tell you the truth I think is some idea blending from both my father's and my mother's heritages. Actually you can throw just about anything together."

Darkness descended early due to the low clouds and they decided to turn in early. Both were a little tired, Bob mostly from the exercise and both from the afternoon of card playing and the gloom of early night fall.

However once in bed, they found sleep to be elusive and both rolled and tossed for some time before falling asleep. Even then their sleep was disturbed by dreams that weren't far apart in their nature.

Chapter 21

Alicia awoke before Bob and taking the wash basin with her, slipped outside to visit the 'johnson bar' then using cold water she bathed as best she could.

When she went back inside, Bob was sitting on the edge of the bed.

"How's the weather out there?" He asked.

"Well the rain has stopped and there is a light mist, but I have a feeling it will clear off."

A brief flicker of disappointment crossed Bob's face but he said, "Oh good, I guess we'll get away this morning then."

They ate a breakfast of canned berries then started preparing for their trip.

Bob had relatively nothing but the clothes on his back to take and Alicia decided to leave her sleeping bag and tent behind, they put Bob's bow and arrows and the few things that they considered of some value down in the dug out beneath the floor and moved the bed back over the trap door.

Bob said at one point, "I'll go up on the roof and put the pee can over the chimney"

"Oh no, not with you still limping," Alicia said. "I'll do that and you can do what ever has to be done in the woodshed."

Bob reluctantly let her clamber up and place the tin.

As Alicia climbed back down Bob went to the root cellar and picked up the remaining cod filet and after a moments hesitation, picked out a few of the larger potatoes. They finished putting together two light packs, rechecked everything inside the cabin and out then shouldering their packs and Alicia carrying her rifle they walked to the edge of the clearing.

Almost as if on cue they both turned and looked back as they reached the trail head. After a moment Bob half whispered, "I am going to miss this place and I want to tell you that I have really enjoyed these few days with you."

Alicia, unexpectedly to them both, stepped close and kissed Bob on the cheek. "I know, me too, I'm glad it was here for you to find." Then she quickly whirled away, "C'mon hopalong let's get going."

They didn't hurry, wherever the trail's width would let them, they walked side by side. They paused for a quarter hour at the spring, Bob pointed out to Alicia the various microclimates on her small island. She was quick to understand and like he had been amazed at the diversity in such a small area. When they reached the beach the tide was high and on a whim they decided to pull Bob's raft up as high as they could get it then tied it so it couldn't get away

They didn't discuss why neither of them
wanted to see it drift away.

The stern of Alicia's boat was just in the
water so the bailed out the rain water that
had accumulated, deposited their packs in
the boat and pushed off from shore.

The outboard started on the second pull and
they headed out into the shallow channel at
slow speed.

As they rounded the end of the island, Bob
called out, "Hey we left your fishing rod at
the tree, do you want to pick it up?"

Alicia instantly altered course and they
angled into the beach and the fishing reef.

As the bow grated on the gravel, Bob got out
and hurried to the tree where the rod had
been left, he scooped up the few lures that
were there along with the rod and went back
to the boat.

"Next time I come, I'll bring them back,"
Alicia said.

Bob nodded, "Good idea."

Alicia restarted the motor and made a sharp
turn and headed north west.

They pulled into Ucluelet harbor in the early
afternoon. As Bob secured the boat, Alicia
said, "You better stay at my place tonight.
You can do all your phoning from there and
have a number where you can be called
back."

Bob looked down at the water for a second, "Thanks, I guess I'll need to if it's okay, I have no money or identification, it would be hard to get into a hotel the way I look."

"Good, that's settled then. I'll run up and get my car while you move all this stuff up to the road. Oh, there is a tarp right there, maybe you could cover the boat please."

Half an hour later they drove away from the dock but instead of going straight to her house Alicia drove to the police station. When Bob looked at her she said, "Thought you should report yourself found and we can leave my phone number with them."

Chapter 22

After a half hour of explaining and a promise to return the next day, Bob and Alicia got back in her car and made the short trip to her house.

After unloading the car, Alicia showed him around then said, "Make yourself at home, if you want to have a shower there are towels under the sink, I'm going to run down to the store and get a few groceries. And I just remembered, there may be some of my Dad's clothes stored in a trunk up in the attic, I'll check when I get back, but I'll also pick up something you can wear, for that you can pay me when you can."

Bob grinned, "A shower you read my mind, and when I get some cash I'll pay you for the grub."

"No you won't, I've been eating your food for most of the week."

"Yeah, I didn't think you would ever get tired of that deer meat!" Bob laughed.

Alicia smile back and went back out to her car.

Bob turned and headed for the bathroom and in minutes was stripped and stepping into the shower. He slowly turned the hot water higher as he showered, enjoying the heat as it increased.

He stayed under for close to ten minutes and had just finished toweling off when he heard Alicia return.

He wrapped the towel around his waist and stepped out into the hall.

"Hey Bob," Alicia called, "I dropped a bag with a few things inside the front door, I hope they'll fit."

He retrieved the bag and returned to the bathroom to get dressed.

He emerged a few minutes later, wearing new underwear, a pair of jeans and a T shirt. As he entered the kitchen, Alicia looked up and smiled, "Hey, that looks better. Everything fit?"

"Yeah, great, pants are a couple inches long but they work just fine rolled up, thanks Alicia."

"Well here's something else; shaving cream, a razor and a tooth brush, you can use my tooth paste. I got a stick of deodorant but I don't know what you like."

"Hmm, I get the hint, okay back I go." He took the bag she handed him and returned to the bathroom.

Ten minutes later he was back, clean shaven with only one small knick, teeth brushed and his long hair pulled back in a small pony tail and secured with a band he found.

Alicia's eyes widened as he stepped back into the kitchen, "My God, there was a face under all that, you are actually a handsome man."

As soon as the words popped out she flushed and looked away so didn't see Bob blush in return.

He laughed however and said, "Yeah you probably tell that to all the derelicts you find washed ashore."

Alicia laughed in return then said, I've put some chops into a marinade, I thought you might like a change from your usual fare. Now lets go up and see what else there is for clothes."

Together they went up and opened another old trunk that lay beside the box that her mothers papers had been in.

They carried it over to where the single light bulb hung from the roof rafters and opened it up.

The top layer was all female clothing but about half way down they found several pairs of men's pants, a couple of shirts several pair of socks and two pair of men's jockey shorts still in their original packing. On the very bottom was a pair of almost new running shoes and a pair of worn slippers.

They tossed it all down to the floor below, then went down to gather it up.

Alicia held the pants up to Bob and exclaimed, "Wow looks like pretty close to the right size and I think the shirts will be close too. Here try the shoes."

Bob sat down on a stool and pulled them on, ""A tiny bit big, but let me try them with a pair of socks." Then a moment later, "Hey almost perfect."

Alicia passed him the slippers which proved to be stretched and fit loosely. "No problem," Bob said, they'll do and I really do appreciate the loan."

"No loan, they are of no use to me, it's a wonder they have never been thrown out."

Bob nodded "Well thanks anyway and a thanks to your Mom for not giving them the heave-ho."

They paused, each wondering what to do next, then Alicia snapped her fingers, "Here, I'll show you the spare bedroom and then maybe you will want to start making some phone calls?"

"Yeah I guess I better."

Alicia lead him down past the bathroom, "There are only two bedrooms, mine is here, but Mom's old room is here," she opened a door, "it's not too feminine as I cleaned everything out and had it painted after she died. There is a phone on that side, you can use that." She turned and went out the door closing it behind her.

Chapter 23

A half hour later Bob came out and found Alicia sitting in the living room reading a newspaper.

She put the paper down as he entered and said, "Well how did it go?"

Bob, looking somewhat emotional, replied, "Well good, they were pretty surprised, thought I was dead of course. I don't have any numbers or anything for anything to do with work, banks or anything so he will get hold of the lawyer that he was working with and start reversing everything that's been put in motion. He was pretty excited." He paused then went on, "He can't get here for a couple of days, so if you want he can arrange for a hotel for me."

"Why would I want that? You will stay right here until he gets here, longer if you want."

"Thanks, Alicia. I did give him the number that was on the phone so we may be getting some calls for me."

"Good, now how about a sandwich? We can sit and talk in the kitchen while I make them."

"Sounds good to me but I have another favor to ask."

"Sure go ahead."

"Do you think we could have a cup of coffee?:

Alicia threw back her head and laughed heartily, "Of course we can and I'll even let you make it."

The next hour went by quickly as they ate sandwiches and drank coffee together at the kitchen table.

Then filling their cups once more they moved back into the living room and continued talking about themselves and asking questions of each other. Slowly they both became aware of how comfortable they were with each other, they said nothing about it but just allowed themselves to enjoy what was happening.

Later they went for a walk around the town, Alicia seemed to know almost everyone they met but made no effort to explain Bob's presence.

"I'll introduce you another day, Bob. There will be a lot of questions eventually and I don't want them to know all about our, uh my island."

"No problem, I don't feel like talking to strangers right now, I think I may have got a bit 'bushed' out there."

They walked on then after a while retraced their steps back to the house.

As they went through the door Alicia said, "Besides coffee, I bet you may have missed the odd drink or two."

Bob smiled, "well I'm not a big drinker but I
noticed you had some wine and I think I
could go a glass."
"You're on, I'll pour us each a glass then I'll
get supper started."
"Is there anything I can do?"
"No just sit, you can turn on the TV if you
want."
"No that's okay, I'll just sit and try to figure
out everything I have to do over the next
while. Have you got a sheet of paper and a
pen I could borrow?"
"In that little alcove off the living room,
there should be paper and pens on the desk."
Bob went out and reappeared a moment
later, pen and paper in hand.
He sat down at the table and watched Alicia
bustle about then bent his head and started
jotting down things as they entered his mind.

Chapter 24

Later after they had finished supper and washed and dried the dishes, Alicia poured more wine and they went back to the living room.

They talked for a bit, reliving some of their island experience and when the conversation slowed, Alicia turned on the television and flipped through the channels. There was nothing that interested either of them and she hit the off button.

After a few moments she said, "Bob? What now? What's next?"

They both realized that the question had double meaning. Bob hesitated for a moment then said, "Well after my brother arrives with some of my personal papers, I'll get all my financial stuff in order; driver's license, credit cards and et cetera. It will mean a trip back home and I thought it over this afternoon, I am going to put my house up for sale." He paused then went on, "After that I'll get another boat, the old one was insured so that'll be covered and then I'm not sure, maybe back to my cabin up island."

Alicia nodded, "Well that will keep you busy for a while."

"Yeah a couple of weeks anyway. What about you, what's next for you?"

"Oh, oh I don't know, I don't feel like going back to my old job, I've given some thought to staying here and opening up my own business, consulting."

"Mm, hmm, that sounds interesting," and before he could stop himself Bob said, "would you like to come up and visit me sometime? Or ah, uh, maybe I could come and see you?"

In the darkening room neither could make out the others face and their flushes were not seen.

Alicia got up and fetched the wine bottle and without asking, refilled Bob's then her own. Standing in front of him she looked down and said, "Bob, I'm not one to beat around the bush. The last few days have been special I finally realized and I have grown to like you – very much. Before I go traipsing off to another isolated cabin with you, I need to know where we are going emotionally."

Bob slowly rose to his feet and looked down at her. "Alicia, I can't answer that, I feel the same way as you, I think you are an amazing woman, the house keeping things I need to do are really nothing, but I still need to come to terms with the loss of my wife. I'm sorry."

Alicia stared up at him, her eyes shiny, "I know, I know and thank you for being honest. Okay let's just wait and see what the future has in store, take things as they come."

She stood on her tip toes and kissed him lightly on the lips then stepped back.

"Okay drink up and let's try that stupid TV again."

They watched a short documentary until the news came on, watched that, then Alicia said, "Well I'm off to bed. Are you staying up?"

"No, I'll turn in too." Bob said and rose to his feet.

They both walked down the hall with Alicia leading the way, she turned at her door and said, "Good night Bob, sleep well."

Involuntarily Bob reached out and took one of her hands, "Alicia, thank you, thank you for everything you've done and for your understanding."

She started to reply but Bob raised his other hand and touched her lips. He leaned forward and when she didn't draw back he kissed her. Alicia started to melt forward then stiffened slightly and drew back, she put a hand to his cheek then turned and stepped through her door closing it behind her.

Inside her room, she leaned back against the door, her chest heaved and her pulse raced. Tears trickled down her cheeks. "Damn, oh damn," she whispered. She stayed like that for a few seconds then straightened and moved across the room.

On the other side of the door, Bob stared at the closed door. His hands shook his mind in a whirl. Then he turned and walked to his room. As he changed into a pajama bottom that Alicia had laid out at some time he muttered aloud, "Yeah Bob what next?"

Chapter 25

They were both up around seven the next morning, they had a light breakfast of cold cereal and several cups of coffee. Bob paced around the house until Alicia asked him to go to the store. "Your brother won't get here before ten or eleven probably, here is a list of a few things I need."

Bob stated to protest but Alicia said, "I'll be here by the phone, if he gets here before you get back I'll be better at telling him how to find my house and you should exercise your hip."

Bob took her list and some cash she handed him, "Okay, and I'm keeping track of what you're spending so you will get paid back." He went out the door and headed for the store.

He was back in about twenty minutes, handed Alicia the bag of groceries and looked mildly disappointed when she told him that no one had phoned yet.

"I noticed that your fence has a bit of a lean out there in front, where will I find a few tools?"

"Out in the back in the garden shed," she replied. "But you don't have to do anything."

"Oh, I know but I want to and it'll pass the time. Besides it looks like it just needs a brace and a few nails."

A little later Bob was just putting the hammer away when Alicia called out, "C'mon Bob, your brother will be here in a moment."

They both went around to the front of the house and sat on the steps.

Bob felt a curious mix of excitement and sadness but waited in silence.

Alicia, unusually talkative, kept up a stream of inconsequential chatter.

They didn't have long to wait until they saw a grey car moving hesitantly along the street. Bob stood up and waved and a moment later the car pulled in behind Alicia's. The first person out was a young girl of about twelve or thirteen followed by an attractive woman probably in her early forties; they both rushed to Bob and embraced him, tears streamed down their faces as they hugged and kissed him. A moment later, Bob's brother stood waiting for his wife and daughter to slow down then stepped forward and the two brothers embraced as well.

Alicia started to cry silently as she witnessed the reunion and started to turn away when Bob's sister in law saw her tears and went to her; "you must be the wonderful heroin we heard about, I'm Irene and this young lady is

Natalie. I think we are very much in your debt."

Alicia blinked back her tears, shaking her head, "No, I am just happy for all of you that this has ended so well, I'm sorry about my tears, it's just seeing you all, y,you, your, oh damn, I'm sorry!" She started to sob.

Irene put her arms around Alicia and said over her shoulder, "Jim, you and Bob have five minutes while Alicia shows me where her bathroom is, then we will all sit down together. Natalie you stay and make sure they come in shortly." She and Alicia moved up the steps and into the house.

While Irene was in the bathroom, Alicia wiped away her tears and set out cups and muffins that Bob had purchased for her earlier.

When Irene came out to the kitchen Alicia was composed and had her emotions in check.

"Can I help?" Irene inquired.

"No, the coffee is made and I'm just setting out these few things. Do you think they will want to be in here or out in the living room?"

"I think here is just fine, that way they can get their elbows on the table and write notes or whatever they think they need to do."

"Are you ready for a cup now?" Alicia asked.

"Please, that would be nice."

Alicia filled two of the cups and together they sat down.

"I'd like to ask you about everything, but I'm sure we will be hearing all about it soon." Irene smiled. "But give me a head start, tell me about you."

"Oh, there's not a lot to tell, I was born and raised here, well actually I was born in Port uh Port Alberni. I went away to school when I was in my teens. Then went to university then work. What about you Irene, are you an island girl?"

Irene smiled again, "Yes, actually I am, I was born in Victoria but when I was nine or ten we moved to Nanaimo and that's where I've been ever since. Met and married Jim and I work part time at a boutique."

The two women chatted for several minutes, both very comfortable with each other.

Finally Irene said, "Okay they've had long enough, I'll go get them."

As she walked to the front, the two men with Natalie attached to one of Bob's arm came through the door.

"Good timing." She said. "We're going to sit in the kitchen."

Before they even sat down, Bob went to Alicia and said, "Jim has got a lot done and everything is done or underway, it looks like it will all be back to normal soon."

Alicia involuntarily put her hand on his arm, "Oh Bob, that's good, I'm so happy for you." She started to raise both her arms but quickly caught herself and turned away. "Sit all of you, coffee's coming. And what about you Natalie? I have coke and ginger-ale or milk?"

"Ginger-ale please." Was the reply.

As they all sat down, Irene, Jim and Natalie all started asking questions at once.

"Hold it, hold it." Bob said. "First things first. Did you bring some money?" He looked at his brother.

"Oh yeah, sorry," Jim pulled an envelope out of his pocket, "here's four hundred bucks."

Bob took the envelope and took out half the money and put in front of Alicia. "That should cover the clothes and things."

"No Bob, that's too much I…."

He cut her off, "Hey, you've fed me and wined me and gave me a boat ride, no it really is too little."

As Alicia started to make a retort, he said, "Please Alicia, just take it, you know that I'll never be able to repay you for all that you've done and I, and I….." He stopped and looked around the table and then simply spread his hands.

Jim and Natalie were both intent on their muffins but Irene had watched both of them

intently from the moment Bob had first gone
to Alicia. Unnoticed a smile played around
her lips and she nodded her head very
slightly.

"Okay," Bob said, "now that's over with I
guess you want to hear our story."

This time Jim looked up sharply at the use
of the word 'our', he opened his mouth to
speak but closed it quickly when he received
a light kick from the direction of his wife.
Bob went on, commencing with the ordeal
of the storm and his awakening on the
beach.

He skipped through a lot of the first few
months and made everyone including Alicia
laugh when he told the part about their first
encounter. At that point she jumped in and
told the story from her perspective.

Before they knew it, the morning had passed
and Bob saying he needed a break declared
that they should go for a walk. "Now that
I've got some money, I'll treat all of you to
lunch down by the water." He said.

Chapter 26

Jim and his family had come prepared to stay the night and had made a reservation at one of the local motels.

After a leisurely lunch at a restaurant that over looked the harbor, Jim and Bob stopped by the motel to get them checked in while the two women and the girl walked on back to Alicia's home.

While they had lunched, the story was continued up to when Alicia had found Bob pinned under the tree.

Intuitively Irene sensed that Alicia had some reservation about telling all the details of the rescue. As they strolled back along the street, she said, "It must have been very traumatic for you when you found him, I don't know how you managed."

Alicia shook her head, "Well yes and no, I just acted on instinct for the most part but the worse was when he was so cold and I was afraid that shock and the cold would, would ah, do ....., oh Irene, I was so scared when I got back, I knew I had to get him warmer, he doesn't know but I stripped down and used my body to warm his."

Irene's eyes widened then she quickly turned to Natalie, "You will not tell either your Uncle or your Father what you just heard, do you understand?"

"Yes Mom, but …."

"No buts, Alicia did a very brave thing and probably saved Uncle Bob's life, she doesn't need to have any embarrassment come her way. Go on Alicia."

Realizing she had suddenly acquired a new and understanding friend, Alicia recounted the events of the following two days.

They reached her house just as she was telling about the events of the morning after the ordeal. "I'll leave it there as from here on Bob was awake and lucid and it gets back to being our story as opposed to the bit while he was out of it."

Irene had listened in silence, tears had come to her eyes repeatedly during the telling and as Alicia ended she reached out and drew Alicia to her. The two women clung to each other for a moment, then both stepped back, teary but smiling.

As they opened the door and went inside, Irene said to her daughter, "I hope your Uncle realizes he has found a gem."

Later they all gathered together in the living room, where Alicia gave a shortened account of finding Bob and getting him to the cabin. Then together they told the remainder of the story. As the story progressed Bob's eyes initially kept finding Alicia's then finally, to their audience, it was as though they were telling their story to each other.

Jim looked at Irene once with a questioning look but she just made a shushing motion and shook her head.

By the time the story tellers were finished and questions answered, it was late afternoon.

Alicia jumped up saying, "Would anyone like a drink? I have wine, some rum and I think a half bottle of gin."

Jim said, "And I have a couple bottles of wine in the car, I think we should have a celebration."

Irene interjected, "Before we start, I'm going to run up to the store. Do you have a barbeque, Alicia?"

"Oh there's an old one out in the shed but I don't think there is any propane. It hasn't been used in years."

"No problem, probably to cold outside for that anyway. I'll pick up something we can do inside."

Alicia said, "I'll go with you and we can shop together. You'll probably like our store, it's sort of 'old country style'."

"You go with your Mom and Alicia, honey." Jim said to Natalie. "Uncle Bob and I have a couple more things to talk about."

Jim went out and brought back his wine and the women headed for the store.

After opening one of the bottles and pouring themselves a glass the two men settled once more in the living room.

"So what else do we need to talk about?" Bob asked.

"Uh well I just, well I'm curious about where you and Alicia are at." Was the reply. Bob flushed then said, "Well first it's really none of your business."

As Jim started to speak again, Bob held up his hand, "Wait I'm not finished. It isn't any ones business but I'm kind of glad you asked. She saved my life, no question, she is really a very wonderful woman and I have grown quite fond of her." He stopped and stared at the floor.

Jim waited a moment then said, "I think I hear a 'but' in that comment."

"Yeah, the 'but' is that I feel guilty or maybe disloyal and I just don't know what to do."

They were both silent for a few more minutes, then Jim said, "Well little brother, she seems to me like a pretty nice girl, I can tell that Irene is taken with her, she's obviously smart and can take care of things. I guess I would advise not to rush but by the same token, don't wait too long, someone else may snatch her up." He paused then added, "There is no reason to feel guilt now or in the future, the past is past. Drink up and I'll pour you another."

Chapter 27

When the women got back they whipped up a meal of fried chicken supplemented by oven heated frozen French fries and a large spinach salad.

Bob and Jim moved into the kitchen and the conversation moved on to what had been happening in Irene and Jim's lives since Bob had been missing.

Later as they ate they talked about random things, Natalie's school year, provincial politics, the price of gas. They joked and laughed and felt the joy of bonding.

Alicia while enjoying and participating kept having moments or twinges of trepidation that she smothered and showed no outward sign.

Later they moved back to the living room and after a little while Natalie started to nod off to sleep, tired from all the excitement and the continuing adult conversations.

Irene noticing said, "Bob maybe we should go it's been a long day for her." She nodded at Natalie.

"No not yet," Alicia exclaimed, "Let her stay here tonight she can slip into my bed, there's lots of room."

Jim looked at Irene, she hesitated for only a second, "Sure that sounds okay. How about

it dear, do you want to stay here with Uncle
Bob and Alicia?"

Natalie nodded, "Sure that sounds like fun,
can I go to bed now?"

In a few minutes she was dressing in a spare
pair of Alicia's pajamas, she came out and
said good night to everyone as she went up
to Alicia she said, "Is it alright if I call you
Aunty Alicia?"

Alicia froze for a second then, "Of course
you can, I would be honored." She couldn't
bring herself to look at Bob.

The adults sat up until about eleven talking
and laughing. Irene after a big yawn said,
"Well Jim, I think we better call it a night.
We have to be away reasonably early
tomorrow and it has been a very full day."

Jim nodded, finished his drink and stood up.
"Yep you're right," he turned to Alicia and
said, "Thank you so much for all you have
done and especially for your part in getting
Bob well and back to civilization."

Alicia stood up as well, "Believe me I am
just happy that I found him and it all turned
out so well. By the way, I'll have breakfast
ready around seven thirty and you can eat
and run."

Good nights and hugs were passed all
around and in a few minutes Bob and Alicia
were alone.

They cleaned up everything and just stacked the glasses and plates in the kitchen sink. Bob wanted to wash them then but Alicia said, "No, I'll have lots of time on my hands tomorrow and there will be breakfast dishes to do as well."

A sad look passed over Bob's face and he turned away and started for the kitchen door; he paused and turned back, "Alicia, I don't know what to say, I actually need to go but I also would like to stay."

She looked squarely at him, "Bob you <u>do need</u> to go. Not just to get your affairs in order but to get your life in order as well. I'm going to be honest again, I would love to have you stay but until your ghosts are laid to rest there isn't room for me in your life or you in mine. I'm sorry."

Bob stared at her for several seconds then nodded, "You're right, I know. But please let's stay in touch, I think I'm still in need of your help."

"You can stay in touch, I will cherish every moment that we can talk, but you must be the one, I, I can't, won't be a persuader, you must reach your own decision."

Bob stepped toward her but she held up one hand, "No Bob, please."

He stopped, held her eyes for a moment then slowly nodded and said "You're right, good night Alicia." He turned and left the room.

Alicia stared blankly after him for a long time and then drew a shuddering breath and started to cry softly.

Chapter 28

The next morning, Alicia slipped out of bed without awakening Natalie, had a quick shower and went out to the kitchen. Bob was already there, He had started a pancake batter and had a dozen eggs on the counter ready for frying, coffee was ready and he had poured her a cup when he heard the shower water stop.

He glanced up as she came in, "Hope you don't mind, but I woke up early."

"Of course not Bob, we can do the cooking together."

Bob said, "About last night…."

"No please let's not go there, when you are ready I'll be here." To herself she said, *'I'll always be here.'*

Jim and Irene arrived a little while later and they all sat at the table drinking coffee.

Irene picked up immediately on the strain between Bob and Alicia but said nothing.

A few minutes later Natalie came out still looking sleepy and Bob started to cook the pancakes.

Alicia put the eggs on after the first batch of pancakes were off the griddle and in short order they were all sitting, talking and eating.

Although Irene had noticed right away that neither Bob or Alicia were eating with any enthusiasm, it was Jim finally who said, "Hey, what's wrong with food, both of you are hardly eating."

Irene gave him a hard look but couldn't give one of her kicks as she was too far away. When no one answered Jim he suddenly lost his grin and colored slightly then bent down to his plate and ate without looking up.

Alicia desperately tried to think of something to restore the fun time but the best she could come up with was, "Well at least it's not raining for your trip h-h-home." She stood up from the table and with her back to it asked in a slightly muffled voice, "More coffee?"

No one wanted any but they all accepted another half cup and whiled away another fifteen minutes or so then Jim said, "Well I think we gotta get going."

"Are you sure we can't help with dishes, dear?" Irene asked.

"No, no of course not. You better get on the road, you'll still be able to get something done this afternoon."

They all went out to the front step, good byes were said and hugs exchanged. Bob hesitantly embraced Alicia for a second and whispered something she couldn't catch. He had nothing to take but the clothes he was wearing and a shopping bag of the extras. He put them in the trunk and started to get in the car, then stopped and leaving the door open went back to where Alicia was standing with her chin up raised.

He reached out, grabbed one of her hands and pulled her back through the open door and kicked it shut behind him.

"I'm sorry." He said hoarsely. He took her into his arms and kissed her firmly on the lips. She stayed rigid for a moment then slowly she melted against him and kissed him back. It was a long kiss broken finally by Bob, "I'm sorry." He repeated. "But I needed to do that, I needed to know what I could lose."

He turned and went out the door, got in the car and said to Jim, "Go, go now!"

EPILOGUE

(i)

Several minor glitches frustrated Bob in the first couple of weeks after he returned home. Because his credit cards had been cancelled some of his bills had not been paid and already three bill collection agencies had been active. In due course he dealt with these and was satisfied that all interest charges were dropped when the circumstance of his situation were made known.

He phoned Alicia two evenings after he had left her at her front door. Their conversation was stilted and very casual in the beginning but became more relaxed after a time.

He made up his mind that he would phone her twice a week but choose not to tell her but to just do it. After the first two weeks she realized what he was doing and made every effort to be near the phone on those evenings.

About a month after his departure Alicia had an offer of a direct short term contract to investigate some bear poaching. She accepted it as it was quite lucrative and she was already very restless with being house bound and even town bound.

She told Bob about it the first evening he phoned after her acceptance and told him she would be away for the next two weeks but would phone him when she got back. When she told him he said, "Jesus Alicia, these guys will have guns, I don't think you should ….!"

She cut him off, "Don't be silly, I'm trained for this stuff, I have an open warrant and I will have guns as well! Besides at this point I'll be only trying to collect evidence."

"Well can't you have a cell phone with you, we could stay in touch?"

"No I can't do that. Don't worry The wildlife folks will know where I am and I will be in touch with them by radio every night."

She changed the subject and said she thought she might stop by the cabin as it was just a little out of her way to where she was going.

"You're changing the subject, Alicia. Just be careful, please be careful."

"I will dar, uh, uh Bob. I'll call you the moment I can."

They talked for a few more minutes during which time Bob told her that his insurance money had come through and he was negotiating for a new boat.

"Oh yeah, I had a job offer doing stream flow analysis from the feds but I turned them down."

"Why did you do that? You can't do nothing forever." Then quickly, "Oh I'm sorry Bob, I shouldn't have said that."

"No, no it's okay, my specialty is coastal streams and tidal interaction and I got a tip that there is something coming along soon. This other one would have put me up in the northern Rockies and would have been unavailable."

Although she felt a surge through her body, Alicia didn't let her voice show her burst of elation. "Oh good, I hope it works out."

"I think it will."

A few moments later they said good night.

(ii)

By the end of Alicia's two week absence,
Bob was almost beside himself with worry.
Finally one Saturday afternoon, she called,
This was the first time she had initiated a
phone call.

"Hi Bob, I'm home." Was her opening when
he picked up his phone.

"Hi, hi are you okay, how did it go, are you
okay?"

She smiled at the other end, somehow happy
at his obvious concern.

"Fine, I'm just fine. It went well, I got all
kinds of evidence including a video of these
two guys taking down a bear and then
cutting out a few things that go on the black
market. I got their boat in the clip and then
later I zeroed in on the carcass. They are
probably being apprehended as we speak."

"Wow! Good for you, I knew you could do
it. But, but I was a bit worried."

Alicia smiled into the phone, "Nothing to
worry about. So what's been happening?"

Well I got the boat and took it up to Tofino,
I listed my house and got an offer on it two
days ago. And I have bid on a long term
contract that covers all the west coast of the
Island and around the north end to the Port
Hardy area."

"Hey, you have been busy. When did you list your house?"

"Uh, well a week or so ago, I guess."

"You guess?"

"Uh yeah, well it was the day after you told me about your contract."

Alicia started to comment, then decided that she should not go there. "So when do you find out about the contract?"

It closes a week today, I heard there were only three bidders, I'm pretty sure I know who they are and they don't worry me much, but anyway I didn't bid really high as I expect I would have much lower overhead than either of the other two."

"Sounds good, I really hope you get it."

"Yeah me too." He paused then said, "Hey Alicia, would you, uh would you like, can you; oh crap, how about coming with me when I go up to the cabin? I haven't been there since I went fishing that day and I know it needs checking out."

Alicia froze for a moment then said, "I, I don't know Bob, how long will you be there?"

"Well if we got away early and the weather was nice, probably just for the day, at the most overnight."

"Well, maybe, give me some time to think it over. When do you plan on going?"

"I can go anytime before this contract is let, actually I had thought about tomorrow or the next day."

"I have a couple of errands to run and groceries to buy, I'll call you back in about an hour."

"Okay, bye for now."

They both hung up.

(iii)

Bob answered the phone on the first ring,
"Hi, what have you decided?"
"Sure I'd love to go, but it's too late in the
day to go tomorrow."
"Uh, well I could leave right now, I'd be at
your place by eight or nine o'clock and we
could leave first thing in the morning. I've
checked the weather and there is no wind
forecast."
"Okay, I'll have a late supper out for you
and I'll pack a picnic lunch for tomorrow."
"Great, we can eat in Tofino when we get
back, it was about an hours run each way in
my old boat, I should be able to shave off a
few minutes with this one."
"Okay Bob, drive safe though."
"Yep, will do, bye."
Alicia bustled around, she decided that as it
would be late, a light supper of a cheese
omelet would be best. She prepared
everything then put it in the fridge to cook
later. Next she made sandwiches and made
up a picnic cooler with the sandwiches, a
couple of apples and a small bottle of white
wine.
Being busy had kept her mind occupied but
when the food preparations were all
complete her mind kicked into gear and her

excitement over seeing Bob and going on the excursion with him battled with her trepidation of what she was doing and her fear of letting her guard down.

"Forget it dummy, you've made your decision, everything will be just fine." She muttered to herself.

Time passed slowly, she paced a bit, tried to watch television, paced some more the said aloud, 'To Hell with it, I'll go for a walk.' She walked down to where her boat was tied, she checked it over even tough she had just returned in it earlier that day. She left and strolled along the waterfront, stopping to talk now and then with people she had known all her life. She stopped by the pie and coffee shop and had a cup of coffee, then on impulse bought a wild huckleberry pie. It was now quarter after seven, so she turned her steps to home.

Ten minutes later she turned off the street into her front yard as she reached her steps a large pick-up truck rounded the corner and sped up the street.

When it reached her house it slowed and wheeled in behind her car. It was Bob! Alicia put the pie down on the top step and without restraint ran to the truck, Bob jumped out, rounded the front and they crashed together in an embrace.

After a few seconds of hugging, Alicia stepped back, "How did you get here so soon, I told you to drive safely!" She scolded.

Bob grinned, "I kept it down except here and there. I had the truck all loaded and ready to go so it was just a matter of shutting the door behind me and taking off."

They started inside then Bob turned back and reaching into the back of his truck, pulled out a small overnight bag. Alicia picked up the pie and they went inside.

"Since you're here, we'll eat earlier. It's all ready to go on the stove. You know where your room is and you can pour us each a glass of wine."

"Ha, well I'm not freeloading this time, I brought along a couple bottles." He took his bag down to the room he had used before and brought back two bottles of Australian Shiraz. He filled the two glasses that Alicia had set out and handed her one, the clinked their glasses together and raised them slightly in a silent toast.

Suddenly in the quiet room they both felt a feeling of perhaps unsureness, or shyness. They both felt it but if asked neither could have expressed it.

They sipped their wine and the intensity of the feeling diminished and in a moment they had moved on and were bombarding each other with questions.

Alicia had the dinner cooked and on the table in short order and as they ate she retold him but in more detail the story of her surveillance of the poachers.

"I'm pretty sure 'the powers that be' were happy so I expect there will be more contracts, there are always poaching incidents all over the island."

Bob suddenly looked thoughtful, "Are they always in a hurry with these things, what if you were tied up with another project?"

"No not always, in the past when I was involved up north, they often were over a period of time and the evidence might involve several instances. Why?"

"Oh, no reason, I was just wondering." But Alicia noticed a tiny frown on his face but left it at that.

They finished their supper, washed and dried the dishes together then moved into the living room with their glasses refreshed. They talked more about the weeks that had passed, then Alicia asked, "What time do you want to get started in the morning?"

Bob replied, "I thought if we left here about five we would be able to get away from the boat launch by sixish and that should give us a full day and time to get back."

"Fine, we both need our beauty sleep, so maybe we should call it a night."

"Okay, don't worry about breakfast, we can grab something in Tofino to take with us."

"If you like, But I'll have coffee to go and I just remembered we never ate the pie I picked up so we could have that for breakfast."

Bob grinned, "Yeah pie for breakfast, I could go for that."

"Okay that's settled. You can have the bathroom first."

"Thanks and by the way, maybe I do but Alicia you don't need a beauty sleep."

Alicia blushed and said, "Don't be foolish, go to bed. I'll set my alarm."

(iv)

Everything went as planned and by quarter after six they were a hundred yards off the Tofino boat launch.

Bob's new boat was a twenty-one foot welded aluminum hull with a small cuddy and aluminum cabin, it was powered by two -two hundred and ten Yamaha motors. He was obviously proud of it. "Under the right conditions, I can probably do at least forty knots." He said with a grin.

There was no surface wind and the normal eight foot swells were well spaced and they made good time. As they cruised along Alicia thought about the change in Bob. Before he had been intense sometimes moody, pain from the soul could often be seen in his eyes.

Now he was relaxed, happy and his inner conflict was either gone or deeply suppressed. The change only made him more endearing.

In forty-five minutes they turned sharply into the beach and what appeared to solid rock, Bob changed direction and then a second time and almost miraculously an opening appeared in the rock, he slowed the boat and they slipped through a narrow channel and into a small bay.

At the head of the bay was a small floating dock and above it poking out of the trees was the front of a cabin that curiously blended into the rocks and the trees over it. They idled up to the float and Alicia jumped out and secured the boat.

Bob shut down everything then climbed out behind her, "Welcome to my cabin, you shared yours and now I share mine."

They walked up the rocky path and Bob opened the unlocked door; to Alicia's questioning look he said, "Well I was only going out for a couple hours fishing."

The inside while reasonably clean was untidy and cobwebs were noticeable in several corners.

"I think I know why you asked me along." Alicia commented.

Bob just grinned and said, "I'm afraid my freezer and the fridge will be a real mess, they run on propane."

The propane had run out, probably months before and when Alicia opened the fridge door she was greeted by the sight of rotted and dried, fruit and vegetables.

"How do we heat water?" She asked.

"I have a couple of spare hundred pound tanks, I'll hook them up."

He went outside and started exchanging tanks; Alicia took off her jacket, rolled up her sleeves and went to work clearing out everything in the fridge. When Bob came back she said, "I'll do the fridge, you look after the freezer." He nodded and went back out to where the freezer was located in a small shed.

They worked until about noon then heated some water and washed up.

The sun had burned off the sea mist and for mid November the outside temperature was fairly comfortable. They sat out on the small verandah and ate their lunch.

(v)

By late afternoon, everything looked to be back in order. After washing the fridge out with baking soda and water Alicia declared it ready to be used again. Bob wasn't so sure about the freezer but after emptying it out and dumping its contents into the bay he washed it out twice with bleach water.

They left the doors for both appliances wide open. Bob shut off the propane and wrestled the two empty tanks down to the float and on to the boat.

When he was finished he said, "Okay good enough. Let's relax a bit then we can head back."

They sat down out side again and finished off Alicia's bottle of wine.

As they sat Alicia studied Bob for a moment then asked, "How long have you had this?" She waved an arm around in a circle.

"I bought the property several years ago and built the cabin two years ago."

Hesitantly Alicia said, "And your wife, did she like it here?"

Bob stared out to the bay for a moment the said, "She was never here, we were going to come but somehow other things got in the way."

Alicia just nodded, she had noted the lack of anything feminine and wondered.

"I'm sorry Bob, she would have loved it."

He shrugged, "Well I'll never know."

Suddenly Alicia shivered, she wished now she hadn't mentioned his wife and hoped she hadn't stepped over a line.

Bob looked at her and read the look of consternation that showed on her face. "It's okay Alicia, it's okay. I've moved on I will always remember but I have moved on.

Bob slowly rose to his feet and stepped to where Alicia was sitting, he reached out and she raised her hand to his. He pulled her to her feet and they moved together in a sudden embrace.

Passion flared in both of them, they kissed each other hungrily, then suddenly Alicia felt the storm in her heart and her body abate and she leaned back in his arms.

Bob looked at her, looked deeply and then nodded slowly. Gently he drew her back and touched his lips to hers.

"The right moment will come, we can wait."

(vi)

A few minutes later they did a 'walk around together and decided that everything was in order. Bob left the door unlocked. It was unlikely that anyone would find his small cove but if someone did and they needed shelter, it would save have the door broken down.

On the way back to Tofino they stopped and jigged for cod and caught two large ones, which Alicia filleted as Bob steered onward for Tofino.

As they pulled the boat out of the water, Alicia asked, "What are you going to do with your boat?"

"I guess I'll take it home with me, it's expensive storing it here and the security could be better."

"Won't that be a hindrance if your house sells?"

"Yeah, but I can deal with it when it happens."

"Why not leave it at my place? It will be safe there and if you are coming over here, it's hardly out of your way."

"Are you sure Alicia? That would be great!"

"Of course I'm sure, we can flush your motors and wash her down in the morning. There's enough room in my yard. One catch though."

"Yeah, what's that?"

"After all my hard labor and using up my yard it'll cost you a dinner."

Bob laughed, "You're on!"

They got the boat backed in and parked by seven o'clock; while Alicia went in to have a hurried wash, Bob washed down the trailer and flushed the boat motors.

He also had a quick wash up and both in a change of clothes were ordering their dinner at the same restaurant that they had gone to with Bob's brother and family.

When they got home, the long day, fresh sea air and a big meal had them both ready to go to bed.

After a quick embrace at Alicia's bedroom door they both tumbled into their beds and slept until after seven the next morning.

They breakfasted on bacon and eggs and several cups of Alicia's coffee. Finally Bob said, "I guess I better go, maybe I've had a phone call about the house."

Alicia nodded, "Yes, maybe." Then she said, "Bob, it's almost the end of the month, would you like to come here for Christmas?"

"Well I had thought about seeing if we could go to Jim's but I think I like your idea better. Sure thing."

"Okay, come a couple of days early. We'll talk on the phone I'm sure and you have to let me know how your contract bid goes." Bob snapped his fingers, "That reminds me, I was going to ask earlier but somehow it slipped my mind. Uh you remember when I asked about your contracts if you were tied up or busy?"

"Yes, I do. Why?"

"Well this one and it is a big one, requires that I have a trained wildlife person involved because of the interaction of streams, the ocean, fish and wildlife. I was wondering, uh hoping, uh, you know. Crap, would you consider working with me on it?"

Alicia stared at him for a long moment, her mind racing. "It sounds interesting, can you send me the particulars?"

"Well I happen to have a spare copy of those with me, I'll leave them with you." He went and got his bag and pulled out a large manila envelope and passed it to her.

"You are a sly dog, Bob Anson. Is it my brains that brought you over here?"

He grinned at her, "Of course what else would I be interested in?"

They both laughed and a few minutes later, they kissed good bye and Bob headed back to Parksville.

(vii)

Bob was humming quietly as he drove by
Kennedy Lake. He was about a half hour or
less out of Ucluelet, his signed contract was
in his briefcase, he had talked to Alicia the
night before when she had reconfirmed that
she would participate in the project, his
house had sold two weeks earlier; he
thought to himself, *'I know it can't get any
better, but I wonder why she wanted me to
come over this morning.'*
When they had talked the night before,
Alicia had suddenly concluded the contract
discussion and had quietly said, "Bob can
you leave tomorrow before noon?"
He had replied that he could as now that his
furniture was in storage and the contract
start-up date wasn't until January 5th, he had
little to do.
"Good," Was her reply. "If I'm not home
when you get here, I'll leave a note."
"Okay see you tomorrow."
He had got away about ten thirty and was
feeling a burgeoning excitement at being
with Alicia again.
He pulled up in front of her house right on
the dot of twelve and immediately spotted a
slip of paper taped to the door.

He got out of the truck and hurried over to the door and took the note down and unfolded it.

Hi Bob: Something has come up and I had to run over to my island. I got your boat uncovered and put a few things in it. I'll watch for you from the signal point, I love you.

He frowned at the note, *'that's odd'*, he thought, *why didn't she wait?'*

He turned the truck around, backed up and hitched up his boat trailer. "She must have been in a hurry, her car's not here." He muttered.

He wasn't sure weather he should be worried or not, but just thought it strange. By one o'clock he was shoving off from the boat ramp. He saw a couple of plastic wrapped boxes in the cubby but didn't examine them.

As soon as the last "GO SLOW sign was behind him he opened up the twin outboards. There was about a two foot surface chop from a south east wind so he had to low down to avoid being bounced around. As he cruised along it suddenly hit him that he didn't really know exactly where the island was. He had seen it on a map and he had looked back a couple of times the day they left together.

Finally he slowed right down trying to find a speed that would match Alicia's probable speed then made allowance for the distance he had already covered. After the first hour he spotted an island that looked like it could be the one but once near by he realized it wasn't. He continued on, now doing a zigzag course that generally took him south easterly. He was starting to get frustrated and even a bit panicky when he spotted a curl of smoke coming from a promontory. He turned and ignoring the chop headed towards it at full speed.

Ten minutes later he could see Alicia's small figure waving from the clearing. When he waved back she turned and disappeared from his view.

He slowed then idled into the beach, as luck would have it the tide was very high and he saw that he would be able to nose right up to the heavy logs that were high on the beach. He unhooked his anchor and packed it to the stern and attached a coil of rope to it, then paying out the rope with one hand he continued in until the bow grounded in the sand just short of the logs. He cut his motors and raised them out of the water, then tied the bow to a tree that curved out onto the beach. Next he pulled and tugged on the anchor rope until it was as tight as he could get it.

Satisfied that the boat would be safe he started to get out when he remembered the boxes and turned to get them but the splashing of pounding feet stopped him and he turned to see Alicia running towards him her hair flying around her head.

He jumped out as she arrived, she leapt into his arms laughing and half crying.

"Oh Bob, I am so stupid, I realized only an hour ago you might not know how to find me!"

Bob laughed. "Me too, but I would have found you eventually fire or no fire."

"C'mon let's go up to the cabin."

"What about, your boxes? One each?"

"No, never mind we'll get them later, come let's go."

They were both a little wet from their water splashed meeting and as they hurried up the trail that they both knew so well a drizzling rain started.

When they got to the cabin, Alicia stopped Bob at the door, "Turn around and close your eyes I'll guide you in."

Bob looked at her quizzically, She grinned, "Go ahead, do as I say."

Bob shrugged and turned around and closed his eyes.

She slowly backed him into the cabin and once inside she said, "Keep your eyes closed but you can turn around."

Bob did as she said then after a few seconds
she said, "Okay open your eyes."
Bob stared in amazement. The cabin was
bathed in the soft glow of several candles;
the old stove was gone and in it's place a
small airtight heater and against one wall
stood a small propane cook stove, an elegant
old table had replaced the pole and plywood
one, the old bed was not there, but one end
of the room was curtained off and a corner
of a bed could just be seen. The table was
set with a white linen cloth, two glasses of
wine were on the table with an open bottle
between them.
"What! How, how the hell did you do all
this!" Bob exclaimed. He walked around the
whole cabin noting other smaller changes,
he peeked into the small bedroom area and
looked back quickly at Alicia when he saw
that it contained a double bed. He saw her
blush in the glow of the candles.
"Merry early Christmas Bob."
Bob smiled and reached into his pocket,
"This has been an unusual day but I just
happen to have an early present for you too
which in its own way will make this a day
that I hope neither of us will ever forget."
Alicia hesitantly stepped forward as he took
out what could only be a ring box.
He opened the box to reveal a stylized ring
of entwined gold strands, it was topped by a

dark blue stone lying in a bed of small diamonds, the stone had been crafted into a shape that looked suspiciously like a huckleberry.

Alicia stared so long at it then at Bob that he finally said, "I hope you li…"

She jumped forward and wrapped her arms around Bob as she cut him off, "Oh Bob it's beautiful, it's beautiful; is it a, a…?"

Bob hugged her tight, "Yes it's an engagement ring, will you …"

"Yes, yes a thousand times yes!"

They stepped back and Bob slipped the ring onto her finger and they embraced once more, this time in unbridled passion.

A long time later as the last candle was guttering out they took their first sip of the waiting wine.

End